HEATING UP

Ruff Justice was changing out of his soaking wet clothes when he heard a woman's voice.

"Don't bother putting on anything," Taylor Cribbs said. "You look fine the way you are."

"It's getting pretty cold out," said Ruff, but he didn't make a move to cover himself.

"Don't worry," said Taylor. "I'll warm you up. I owe you that much at least." Slowly the red-head unbuttoned her blouse to expose her gorgeous body. Taylor saw Ruff's eyes spark and she laughed. "Of course, you might have to return the favor."

A moment later, they were on his blanket . . . and suddenly it was damn hard for Ruff to remember there was a killer out in the cold night hot on his trail. . . .

Wild Westerns by Warren T. Longtree

RUFF JUSTICE #25

Jack of Diamonds

by
Warren T. Longtree

Ⓢ
A SIGNET BOOK
NEW AMERICAN LIBRARY

PUBLISHER'S NOTE

This novel is a work of fiction. Names, characters, places, and incidents either are the product of the author's imagination or are used fictitiously, and any resemblance to actual persons, living or dead, events, or locales is entirely coincidental.

NAL BOOKS ARE AVAILABLE AT QUANTITY DISCOUNTS WHEN USED TO PROMOTE PRODUCTS OR SERVICES. FOR INFORMATION PLEASE WRITE TO PREMIUM MARKETING DIVISION, NEW AMERICAN LIBRARY, 1633 BROADWAY, NEW YORK, NEW YORK 10019.

The first chapter of this book appeared in *Flame River*, the twenty-fourth volume of this series.

SIGNET TRADEMARK REG. U.S. PAT. OFF. AND FOREIGN COUNTRIES
REGISTERED TRADEMARK—MARCA REGISTRADA
HECHO EN CHICAGO, U.S.A.

SIGNET, SIGNET CLASSIC, MENTOR, PLUME, MERIDIAN AND NAL BOOKS are published by New American Library,
1633 Broadway, New York, New York 10019

First Printing, April, 1986

1 2 3 4 5 6 7 8 9

PRINTED IN THE UNITED STATES OF AMERICA

RUFF JUSTICE

He knew the West better than any man alive—a hostile, savage land rife with both violent outlaws and courageous adventurers. But Ruff Justice had a sixth sense that kept him breathing and saw his enemies dead. A scout for the U.S. Cavalry, he was paid to protect the public, and nobody was faster at sniffing out a killer, a crook, a con man—red or white, at close range or far. Anyone on the wrong side of the law would have to reckon with the menace of Ruff's murderously sharp stag-handled bowie knife, with his Colt pistol, and the Spencer rifle he cradled in his arms.

Ruff Justice, gentleman and frontier philosopher—good men respected him, bad men feared him, and women, good and bad, wanted him with all the wildness of the Old West.

1

It was a pretty little house south of town. It sat on a small knoll where golden stubble caught the morning sunlight. Crows hopped in the mown grass, competing with each other raucously. The Missouri River flowed past serenely, deep blue and silver in the early light.

Ruff Justice stood inside the house looking out the window. His hands were on the sill as he leaned against the window frame. He was naked from the waist up.

Naked from the waist down.

He yawned and leaned farther out. There was no sign of Amy. She had gone out to feed the chickens and had disappeared.

Ruff looked a little longer. He felt like spending the spring day in bed, and it wasn't going to be much fun alone.

Yawning again, he pulled away from the window, crossed the braided rug on the floor, and went toward the kitchen. He heard the dishes clattering, the soft humming of a woman before he reached the doorway.

When he entered the kitchen, he stopped, content

just to watch for a while as the young blond woman moved around the room doing her work.

She kept her back to Ruff, which was fine. She wore nothing but an apron, and it was delightful to watch her stretch and bend as she put the dishes away in the cupboard. Her hair reached to her waist—glossy, silky, and corn-gold. Her bottom was nicely rounded, blemish-free, taut.

Ruff walked up behind her and put his arms around her, taking her breasts. His body pressed against that exquisite rear, fitting in the cleft of it nicely.

She leaned her head back against Ruff's shoulder and made a small sound of pleasure.

" 'Morning," she said.

"What'd you get up for?" He kissed the nape of her neck, and she pressed against him, holding his hands on her full, firm breasts.

"There's work to do."

"How much work that won't wait?" Ruff Justice asked. The woman turned to him.

"Plenty that's been put off since you got here, if you must know." She laughed. She kissed him once deeply, her lips supple and moist.

"There'll be another day. Come to bed, Amy."

The woman sighed a little and cocked her head to one side. "When are you going to learn my name? It's not *Amy*. My name is Emily, Ruffin T."

"Emily then," he replied, kissing her again, his hands going behind her to caress that smooth, most appealing bottom. "Come to bed, Emily."

"Go along, I'll be in soon," she said, kissing the tip of his nose. "There's only a few more dishes to put away."

"I'll wait in the parlor."

"Wait where you like." She smiled. "That impatient, are you?"

"Afraid so."

"Well, all right. I'll hurry. Now leave me alone so I can get something done."

Justice let his hands drop. He put them behind his back and kissed her once more lightly. He was rewarded with a warm, promising smile.

He walked back to the parlor and returned to the window to watch the peaceful scene. Two crows had gotten ahold of the same field mouse, and they were trying to fly with it in opposite directions. It wasn't working out real well.

Ruff blinked. Emily had gone outside, damn all. The blonde had put on a cotton wrapper and was walking down the slope, along the flagstone path behind the house.

Justice leaned farther out the window.

"Where are you going now? I thought you were coming to bed!"

"In a minute," she called back, waving a hand. "First I've got to feed the chickens."

Ruff waved back, folded his arms, and watched until she had disappeared into the oak trees. This was getting to be a job.

He sat on the settee for a time, arms stretched over the back of it, long legs crossed. Hearing the back door open and click shut, he rose and returned to the kitchen. Amy stood there, a bucket in hand.

"You *are* impatient." She laughed.

"Get the chickens fed?"

"The chickens. Damn the chickens," she said, tossing her head. "I've got to finish these dishes, and I'm not going to make it if you don't scoot." She put her hands on his shoulders and pushed him bodily from the room. "Scoot!"

Ruff muttered something under his breath about women and went to the big airy bedroom. He crawled under the sheets of the big double bed and lay, hands behind his head, watching the door impatiently.

It was five minutes more before the door of the bedroom opened and the blonde came in. She was smiling softly, pushing the door shut with her bare foot as she untied the belt of her wrapper and let it slip from her shoulders, uncovering full, pink-tipped breasts. Ruff's eyes combed the woman, and she stood there enjoying it, liking the knowledge that she was stirring his manhood.

"If you don't get into this bed in thirty seconds, woman . . ." Justice began.

She made it in five, scooting in beside him, her lips finding his, her thigh going over his leg, her hand dropping to his crotch to encircle his thickening shaft.

The door burst open.

Emily stood there accusingly. "So you couldn't wait while I did a few dishes," the woman said. She was untying her apron, and it dropped to the floor, exposing a lush nude body.

"Emily . . ." the woman in bed started to explain.

"Be quiet, sneak," Emily answered.

Ruff Justice lifted up the other side of the sheet, and Emily slipped in to join her twin sister in bed. He looked from one to the other as Emily's hand joined her sister's as she began softly toying with his manhood. He gave it up—he would never be able to tell the two apart—and got busy enjoying them to the fullest.

The flatboat sat motionless in the shade of the huge

dark oaks. The windows of its small, square cabin were covered with black curtains. Ducks moved in a wavering wedge overhead as the tall man in black swung down from his buckskin horse and walked to the river.

He crossed the plank warily. He was no riverman, no sailor. He stood on the deck of the boat, tugging off his black leather gloves. His narrowing eyes caught sight of the other horses tied back among the oak brush. He recognized the silver saddle on the sorrel and frowned.

Jud Hollister always worked alone, and if that wasn't Wiley Pabst's rig he was crazy. He tucked his black gloves neatly behind his gunbelt and walked to the cabin door, rapping on it once.

The woman summoned him inside.

Jud Hollister was a tall man, and he had to duck to clear the door. When he straightened up again, he found himself in near darkness.

Two men sat at a small round table. Wiley Pabst looked up with his one good eye, his whiskered face smirking. Beside him was another familiar face.

Scarred, big-shouldered, the third man's hair was raven-black and straight, sawed off unevenly between the shoulder blades. They called him the Apache, and he looked to have Indian blood in him, but he had the bluest eyes Jud Hollister had ever seen.

"Take a seat," the woman said. She could have been any age, from her voice. There was no other hint. She wore a black dress, elbow-length black gloves, and a black veil which revealed nothing. A lantern with a green shade hung low over the table.

"I asked you to be seated, Mr. Hollister," the voice said from behind the veil.

"I don't know what's going on here," the tall man

replied, "but it looks like it's not up my alley. I always work alone, lady."

"You will work alone. *If* you work. Now sit down." She glanced at the others. "I see Mr. Hollister needs a small inducement."

A gloved hand reached below the table somewhere and came up filled with gold double eagles, which glittered coldly in the lantern light. She spread these out on the tabletop, and Hollister, doing some rapid calculating, figured that there was three hundred dollars or so there.

It was enough inducement.

Jud Hollister pulled up a chair to sit at the table, the chair legs scraping the decking.

"What I propose—" the woman began. She was interrupted as Jud Hollister reached across the table to collect the double eagles. "I see Mr. Hollister is a man who plays it safe," the woman said.

"Always, lady, that's why I'm still alive."

Pabst turned his head and spat, and Hollister tensed briefly. He never had liked Wiley and had always figured that one day when work was short they just might get together and have it out between them.

The Apache hadn't moved. His hands were flat on the table, and Jud Hollister was glad to see them there. The man was unpredictable, as wild as any true Apache, given to black moods. He showed no gun, but Jud Hollister knew that the Apache had a knife hung on a rawhide thong down the back of his shirt. He could reach up behind his neck, find the knife, and throw it with deadly accuracy faster than most men could hope to draw a gun.

Most men. Hollister knew he could beat the Apache, but he had no cause to try.

The woman let Hollister stack and count his gold coins before she spoke.

"I understand you three know one another, so I won't waste time on introductions. And you don't need to know who I am; you work for gold, not for people. I've sent for the three of you because I've been told you're the best at what you do, and that's what I want—the best. Only the best will do."

"Get to the point, lady," Wiley Pabst growled.

"Very well. I have a certain job in mind. One of you, whom I will shortly select, will do this job. The other two will wait."

"Wait for what?" Hollister asked.

"Wait, in case something goes wrong. I don't mean to take any chances. This job *will* get done. The two who will wait here are being paid the same as the man who goes, so you've nothing to lose."

Hollister shrugged. The woman was crazy, but she had plenty of gold to waste. A deck of cards appeared in the lady's gloved hands. She shuffled them clumsily and put the deck on the table, fanning it out.

"Chance will determine which of you gets the job, gentlemen. Mr. Pabst, take a card if you will."

Shrugging, Wiley Pabst stretched out a red, freckled hand, selected a card, and flipped it faceup. Seven of spades.

"Now you," the lady said to the Apache. Expressionlessly he complied, turning up the ten of clubs. "And you, Mr. Hollister."

Jud Hollister's fingers ran over the cards and chose one. He flipped it up and looked at the woman.

"Excellent," she said, touching the card with a gloved finger. "Jack of diamonds. The job is yours, Mr. Hollister. You are the one who will kill Ruff Justice for me."

2

Jud Hollister waited for morning before he started upriver toward Bismarck. He spent the night in the oak grove beside the Missouri not far from the flatboat. He sat beside his small fire, drank coffee and whisky, and thought. As he thought, he cleaned his guns—two Remington .44s with the trigger guards cut off and the action lightened—that were heavily engraved and inlayed with silver. Aside from a fast horse, they were the only thing Jud Hollister had ever spent a lot of money on. But a man in his line of work needed good guns and a good horse.

He checked the loads in his right-hand gun again, closed the gate, and holstered it carefully. The exposed triggers on the Remingtons were a little touchy. He didn't want one hanging up on holster leather and blowing his foot off.

They didn't hang up coming out. Jud Hollister's theory was that having no trigger guards saved him a split second over men with ordinary guns. Maybe there was nothing to the theory—some people told him there wasn't—all Jud knew was that he was still walking around and the men he had faced with factory guns were dead.

He poured himself half a cup of black coffee and shoved the blue enamel, fire-smoked pot back into the embers, filling up the rest of the tin cup with whisky and leaning back against the peeled oak log behind him, one leg drawn up, thinking.

The best time to do it's when he's asleep, Hollister thought. He didn't like that kind of work, but this had to be a sure thing. Hollister's usual method was to get his victim mad, in a blind rage. Drunk and mad if possible—and that was the way it usually worked. They got mad, had a few drinks, grabbed for their guns, and came looking for Hollister.

"Nothin' to that," he said to himself, sipping the whisky. He still had his black hat on, tugged low. Now he took it off and tossed it aside.

There was nothing to getting a man mad. If he had a wife or a woman, that was the best way to go about it. Call her a whore. Call his mother a whore. Or tell him he isn't a man at all—not many could take that.

Justice was another story.

This Ruff Justice wouldn't lose his temper like that. If he had a woman, Hollister knew nothing about her. Justice would have to be approached some other way. He was a dangerous man.

In his sleep would be the best, but if he was an army scout, he likely slept in an army barracks. How the hell could you get a man there and make an escape?

"It's easy when they're eating," Hollister told himself. An ember popped as a spark flew from the fire, and Hollister's eyes followed it into the darkness.

When a man's eating, he's using both hands, with all his attention on his plate. Hollister had taken one man while he was eating. Put the muzzle of his right-hand gun behind his victim's skull while he dug into a bowl of bread pudding.

Never even knew it was coming, Hollister thought, chuckling at the memory of that man's face being blown forward into his bowl of bread pudding.

But Justice would be eating at the army post as well. This would take a little more thought. He needed something new. Something to draw him out and put him in a spot where he could be taken by surprise.

Because Hollister wanted him dead. The lady on the flatboat had another seven hundred dollars for him if he got Justice. That made a thousand in gold altogether. So Ruff Justice would die. It might take a little extra thinking, a little extra time to set it up nicely, but Hollister had time. The lady in black didn't seem to be in any particular hurry. She just wanted to be sure it got done.

It was costing her a bundle to pay Hollister, Pabst, and the Apache to do the same job. The lady must hate hard. What, Jud Hollister wondered, could Justice have done to her?

There was no figuring that, so he drained his cup, kicked out his fire, and curled up to sleep, dreaming of showering gold coins.

Ruff Justice was dreaming different kinds of dreams, and when he woke up they got even better. Softly snoring, Amy was at his left, her thigh over his; Emily was at his right, her yellow hair a tangled mass of gold across her pale shoulders and pink-tipped breasts.

He sighed, yawned, and rose, managing to leave them both asleep. It wasn't the sort of situation a man wanted to leave, but he was already a day behind schedule.

Yesterday he hadn't been able to tear himself away, damn the army.

Still, he knew there was more to life than women—

maybe—and he had been told that Colonel MacEnroe was looking for him. Looking for Ruff—his rambunctious, unpredictable, romantic, and deadly civilian scout.

It could damn well be important. Maybe Stone Eyes had made his way back into the area. The Cheyenne renegade was raising all kinds of hell up north and was said to be drifting south.

Justice stood for a moment in the golden dawn light looking at the two women; cursing himself for a fool, he walked out of the bedroom, snatching up his buckskins.

He dressed in the cold of the kitchen and found his hat beneath the settee where he and the twins had held a small enjoyable party two days earlier. The hat was flat as a pancake.

He buckled on his gunbelt, automatically checking its five loads, and shifted the belt so the Colt rode above his hip, the stag-handled bowie knife behind him. With a last look of regret toward the bedroom, he walked out into the frosty early morning air. He went to the barn, saddled his spotted pony, and rode out toward Fort Abraham Lincoln across the river from Bismarck, Dakota Territory.

The colonel was only furious.

"Where the hell have you been, Justice. You're twenty-four hours late reporting! I've had people out checking with all your known . . . associates."

"Sorry," Ruff Justice said. He sat down on a hard wooden chair in the corner of Colonel MacEnroe's office. He crossed his long legs, placed his hat on his knee, and waited while MacEnroe, lean and silver-haired with a gray mustache clipped military-style, got over his pique.

"I don't know why we continue to pay for your services," MacEnroe said, taking the bottle of bonded bourbon from his desk drawer and filling his coffee cup halfway.

But the colonel knew damned well why the army in Dakota continued to keep Ruffin T. Justice on its civilian rolls.

He was the best.

MacEnroe had Indian scouts that could track better; he'd had other white scouts who knew the area well enough and were far more reliable than this flamboyant, long-haired man in buckskins. But he didn't have anybody with the sheer determination, the guts, the magic needed to stay alive for long on the Dakota plains, while doing the job the U.S. Army gave him to do, come hell or high water.

The whisky or the moment of reflection cooled the colonel's temper a little. He leaned back in his chair and said, "Nothing to this one."

Ruff thought he had heard that once or twice before.

"Then you don't need me."

MacEnroe's frown returned. "You're the natural choice. I want you to take a party of settlers through to Deadwater."

"Deadwater?"

"That's right. Deadwater, on the Flame River." The colonel was briefly silent. It hadn't been long since they had traveled to the Flame together, since the colonel had lost a good woman up there. A woman who loved him.

"There must be someone else," Ruff Justice said. "It's not much of a run—"

"It is for this pack of greeners, Ruffin," the colonel said, his tone softening. His gray eyes twinkled. "I've got bakers and blacksmiths and a grocer, cardsharps and a few women of questionable virtue; I've got a would-be hotel keeper, a stableman, *four* cooks, half a dozen ranch hands, a saddlemaker, and a handful of sodbusters."

"None of them knows which way is west."

"That's about it," MacEnroe admitted. "The Swamp Cheyenne are back on their reservation, content with their lot, it seems, and Stone Eyes is out of the area. It's a garden stroll through to Deadwater, but half these people don't know how to hitch an ox to a wagon. I've been asked for an escort—I can't spare an escort, and they shouldn't need one. I can spare a guide."

"Me."

"You, Ruffin."

Ruff scratched his chin and shrugged. Deadwater was a ghost town at the moment. The woman that owned it, along with the whole mountain valley, was named Susan Donner. She and Ruff Justice had been more than friends; she was a beautiful thing in her early twenties. She had deep blue eyes surrounded by dark, long lashes and reddish-gold hair. She had fallen for Ruff once, but things hadn't worked out, and she had set her sights on a soldier, a man named Mike Drew who was a hell of a warrior, a hell of a man.

"She's bringing that place back to life, is she?" Ruff Justice asked.

"She is. As you know, her father left her an empty town. Susan Donner has decided to fill it up with people. The railroad's going through soon, and it's the natural stop for water and wood, for overnight accommodations.

"Susan's put ads in the Eastern papers for tradesmen and shopkeepers, for milliners and cowboys. She wants to repopulate Deadwater, build it up like her father did. This time, with the railroad committed to go through, it looks like the town will live."

Justice was silent. This wasn't his kind of assignment. It was much too safe, too quiet. Anyone at all could have taken the wagon train through to Deadwater. There had to be something else to it, and he couldn't figure what it was until he asked the colonel, "Any chance of big Mike Drew going along on this?"

"None at all."

"I thought with his hitch about up and Susan waiting . . ."

"Mike Drew's dead," the colonel said. "A small war party, some of Stone Eyes's people, drifted farther south than anyone thought. They came up on Drew's patrol. This time we won—there was only one casualty. Mike Drew."

"So I'm elected to tell Susan Donner," Justice said bitterly.

"You were close to her . . ."

" Close enough to hurt her," Justice shot back.

"That's the assignment, Justice!" MacEnroe exploded. "Do it or pick up your pay and get off the post."

"Again?" Justice said with a small grin, and the colonel gradually relaxed. "I'll do it, sir, but you know there's a lot of assignments I'd prefer. Give me a small war or ask me to get Stone Eyes's scalp. . . . I hate like hell having to tell Susan Mike is dead."

"I don't know what else I can do for her, Ruffin. I could write one of those meaningless official letters, but it wouldn't soften the blow. I sometimes think those letters are nothing more than an added irritant."

MacEnroe didn't need to tell Ruff that he would

hardly be able to write such a letter. He had always hated that particular task, and he and Mike Drew, Susan Donner and Ruff had been through a hell of a lot. Justice supposed the colonel was right. The only way to do it was personally, but there just wasn't any good way to tell a woman that her man has been killed.

"Where are the wagons?" Justice asked, rising.

"Across the river. Thirty-wagon train. It's a fine bunch of specimens, too. Susan's trying to repopulate that town, but looking at this lot it's hard to figure what kind of town Deadwater will be."

The same as any other, Ruff Justice guessed. Drinkers, brawlers, prudes, and intellectuals, hardworking men and women, ne'er-do-wells, and out-and-out crooks. The soft ones would give it up and go back East. The bad ones would get themselves hung.

"One other thing, Ruff," the colonel said, following Justice to the door of his office. "There's a lady who's been looking for you. A lady from the wagon train."

"Yes?" Ruff's eyebrows drew together.

"Not your type. An older woman named Caffiter. Mary Caffiter, I think."

"Caffiter . . . ?" Justice had only known one Caffiter in his time. Billy Lane Caffiter—a blond, blue-eyed, swaggering killer. At eighteen he'd had four notches on the grips of his Colt pistol. At nineteen he was dead, killed by a storm of lead pushed through the barrel of Justice's gun. The little bastard had tried the wrong man, and he'd paid the price.

"You know her?" the colonel asked.

"I'm not sure. Maybe." Mary Caffiter wasn't someone Ruff wanted to meet. MacEnroe knew nothing about the shoot-out in Pueblo, Colorado, and Justice didn't feel like reliving it just then. "Maybe so," was all he said. Then with plenty to think about, Ruff went out, nodding to the huge first sergeant, Mack Pierce, who lifted one slow, heavy hand in farewell.

Outside the sky was blue, the air cold, the post alive with activity. A smith's hammer rang, a small patrol had begun to move out through the front gate, and men were making their way toward the mess hall.

Justice stood on the plank walk in front of the orderly room, thinking that he had come back to Fort Lincoln not twenty-four hours late but twenty-four hours early.

He had no desire to meet Susan Donner with the news he was carrying, no desire to meet this Mary Caffiter if she was related to Billy Lane.

What he wanted was the soft comfort of Amy and Emily, a lazy bed, and golden sunlight coming through the windows.

What he was going to get was an entirely different matter.

Justice swung up onto the back of his spotted horse and rode to the sutler's store for a few supplies. He hardly noticed the tall, dark man in black leather who watched him cross the parade ground.

3

The camp where the would-be settlers of Deadwater were located was a scene of confusion, boredom, anxiety, and anger. Ruff Justice rode slowly through the camp, thinking that he had never seen such an ill-equipped, unprepared group. MacEnroe hadn't been exaggerating much when he said that half of them didn't know how to hitch their oxen to their wagons.

A flaxen-haired kid of eleven or so was chasing a hoop when Justice called to him, "Who's in charge of this outfit?"

"Huh?" The kid turned uncomprehending eyes toward Justice.

"Where's the wagon boss?"

"I don't know what you mean, mister," the kid shouted, and then he was off again, rolling the hoop toward the silver-blue Missouri beyond the oak trees.

Ruff Justice walked his spotted horse forward through the chaos. Some people were trying to unhitch their teams; others were trying to hitch them. He saw one wagon rolling toward the river. The woman on the bench seat didn't seem to know where the brake was.

The Mexican squatting in the shade looked a little

sharper than most of the others. He was prodding a small fire over which a quart can of beans was suspended.

"Who's the wagon master here?" Justice asked.

Dark, wary eyes met his. "We got none."

"That doesn't make any sense. Haven't you elected someone to take charge?"

The Mexican shrugged. "Who? No one here knows what to do anyway."

"How about you?" Justice suggested.

"Me?" The dark eyes flashed. "Who would listen to a greaser? Besides, I have no taste for it."

"What is it you do for a living?"

"Many things," the Mexican said with a wide white smile. "Just now I am planning on being a hostler. I have a few tools, a few horses, much knowledge. I understand there is an empty stable at Deadwater needing a man to run it."

"There is," Justice affirmed.

"You know Deadwater, señor?"

Ruff shrugged. "Well enough, anyway."

"And the woman who owns the town?"

"I know her. If you're worried about Susan Donner, don't waste your time. She's one of the best. Straight as they come. There's no gimmick in her wanting people in that town."

"That is magic to my ears," the Mexican said. "A man reads the paper—or has it read to him"—he grinned—"and thinks, here is a chance. But who knows where the truth lies in these times? Perhaps there is a trick."

"No trick. I'll explain the history of the place sometime if you like. I'm Ruff Justice, hombre, what's your name?"

"Ortega. Felipe Ortega," the hostler said. "There is

one man here who thinks he is in charge. A big man with a red face. McCulloch is his name. He is over there, near the broken oak."

"Thanks . . . one more thing. Seen a woman called Caffiter here?"

"If I have seen her, I do not know her name. A wise man keeps his own company."

"When he's a greaser."

"Yes." Ortega grinned again. "When he is a greaser."

Justice moved on through the camp. He found McCulloch swearing proficiently at a balky team of horses. McCulloch was even bigger than Ruff had expected; he was trying to back his team into their traces but wasn't having any luck at all. The problem was simple and obvious. His saddle horses were unused to the harness and completely ignorant of what was expected of them.

"Are you McCulloch?" Justice asked.

"Who wants to know."

"Ruff Justice. Colonel MacEnroe sent me out to guide you people through to Deadwater."

"Where's the rest of 'em?" the red-faced man asked, taking off his hat to wipe off his forehead with his shirt-sleeve.

"The rest of who?"

"Soldiers? MacEnroe said he'd provide an escort—you can't be it."

"Looks like I am."

"Damn it, what about the Indians?"

"There hasn't been much activity in this area," Justice told him. "Most of the fighting's up north near the Canuck line."

"I still don't like it." McCulloch looked the long-haired, buckskinned man up and down, obviously thinking that Ruff was a poor substitute for a cavalry patrol.

"They tell me you're in charge," Justice said, although it wasn't exactly what Ortega had told him.

"I guess so . . . maybe."

"Someone has to be. If you're not wagon boss, you people should hold an election of some kind. You'll need to be a little more organized than you are."

"You're telling me." McCulloch had relaxed a little. "This ain't an ordinary wagon train, though, is it, Justice? Usually folks sign up with a company and pay money for the privilege of being bossed around by some wagon master. Us"—he shrugged—"we're just a bunch of people who answered a newspaper ad or saw a poster down by city hall. Who is this Susan Donner anyway? Why didn't she organize this thing better?"

"She's just a lady trying to build a town. She's given you an opportunity, it looks like—maybe she couldn't do any more." Ruff asked, "What is it you do, anyway?"

"Hardware. I went bust back in Kansas. Wasn't my fault. Flood washed the whole damn town away last year. Deadwater . . . ?"

"It's high ground," Justice said with a grin.

"Good. According to the rules we agreed to, we all got to wait another twenty-four hours here, you know."

"Another twenty-four hours." Ruff's lips compressed. And the colonel had practically dragged him out of bed.

"That's it. The announcements said gather at Bismarck, Dakota Territory at or before noon on the seventh. I happen to know there's more folks in town trying to find wagons and teams—and they're getting to be in short supply, believe me. I saw you looking at my horses. I ain't quite as dumb as you might think—I know they're not a decent team. But they were the best I could come up with."

"Yeah. Maybe I'll go into town and see if I can help anybody out. Does anyone have space to share in a wagon?"

"Some of us do," McCulloch said, stiffening, "but there's people going along a man don't want to share with."

"Like?"

"Like this gambler, this man called Tibbits. What's he tagging along for? Whatever kind of town this Susan Donner is building, she don't want the likes of him in it."

"Which one's he?" Ruff asked, looking around.

"I don't see him . . . yeah, there he is. Little pudgy man over there. Face like a kid's. Don't let that fool you, he's a real sharper with the cards."

"Maybe someone will give him a lift anyway. At that meeting you ought to try to get everyone who doesn't have a wagon a ride. You can stand most anybody for a few days."

"Not *them*," McCulloch said, and for a moment Ruff didn't know what he meant. Then he saw them; saloon girls, wearing bright clothes and tiny hats, swinging reticules. They were perched on their trunks, watching Justice and McCulloch.

"See what I mean?" McCulloch said, shaking his head, "what the hell kind of town is she building? She was asking for hardworking men and women, craftsmen, cowhands, merchants. She wasn't asking for no whores."

"No. There's always going to be a few tagalongs, though. Besides, McCulloch, you know they'll drift in anyway once the town gets started."

Ruff was trying to placate McCulloch, but he would have none of it. "They might drift in, but they're not going with this wagon train."

"Hold on, now. Nothing gives you that kind of authority. They'll go with the rest of you. Let Susan or whatever law you people set up sort them out. Nobody's playing judge here."

"If I'm wagon master . . ."

"If you're wagon master you'll do your best to organize the people—all of them—and get them through to Deadwater." Ruff said.

But McCulloch wasn't happy. He was the type of man who would never be happy. He just stood with his arms folded, staring at the women.

"McCulloch," Justice asked, "you got a woman named Caffiter here?"

"Mary Caffiter?" McCulloch said.

"That's right."

"Sure," McCulloch said. The anger was still on his face. "Tiny older woman, wears gingham and bonnets."

"Sounds like it could be her. Which one's her wagon?"

"Last one south on the river. Friend of yours?"

"I don't know," Ruff Justice replied. "I mean to find that out."

Perplexed, McCulloch frowned, put his hat back on, and got to work trying to settle his horse team. Justice swung his spotted pony southward and rode past the saloon girls, drawing a whistle and a wink, before he found Mary Caffiter's wagon.

It wasn't in very good shape. The wood was gray and splintered, and one rear wheel appeared to be warped. Justice swung down and hitched his reins to the wagon.

"Mary Caffiter?"

There was no answer, and a peek inside told Justice the wagon was empty. He turned at the sound of approaching footsteps. A tiny woman carrying two huge wooden buckets of water staggered toward him. Justice walked to her and took one of the buckets. Shaded by its bonnet, her pale face peered up at him with surprise.

"Mary Caffiter?" Ruff asked, touching his hat.

"Why, that's right."

Her voice was small and distant, her tiny wrinkle-framed blue eyes questioning. Ruff poured the bucket of water into a barrel on the side of her wagon and replaced the lid.

"I'm Ruff Justice," he said.

The woman clutched at her throat. Her eyes went hard, her mouth puckering.

"You're the one who killed my son, Billy Lane."

"I'm the man he tried to kill, ma'am."

She looked at him for a long minute, then with a tight little shake of her head she spun on her heel and walked away, one of the buckets falling to the ground to roll under the wagon.

Ruff watched the set of her back, the expressive hunch of her shoulders beneath the faded blue gingham dress. He crouched, recovered the bucket, set it on top of the water barrel, and swung aboard his spotted pony, aiming it back toward Bismarck.

Bismarck was busy. Lumber wagons rolled along the main street, spewing dust everywhere. A barefoot kid was hawking newspapers. The saloons rang with noise; the stables were just as active.

The new one, Horner Brothers stable, was completely besieged with people bargaining for horses and fighting over nonexistent wagons. Justice watched from horseback for a while and then swung down, walking around to the back. He left the spotted horse at the hitchrail, hoping no overeager settler would steal it.

He rapped at the back door and got a gruff response. "Go around the front like everyone else."

"It's Ruff Justice, Henry."

A groan, a creaking chair, and then the sound of floorboard heavily trod. Henry Horner was matched only by Mack Pierce for sheer bulk of body. The big man, matchstick in his teeth, opened the door and grinned.

"Come in, but make it quick, Ruffin. They'll make a rush at the door."

"You got horses in your office, Henry?"

Henry Horner's grin broadened, "No, but they might think I do. I haven't seen anything like this since they found that gold in the Black Hills. Greeners, ladies alone, shifty-looking characters in town suits, cowboys, and who knows what . . . all of 'em wanting horses or teams or velocipedes. What in hell's going on, Ruffin?"

Ruff told him. "Remember Deadwater, the ghost town out along the Flame? It's not going to be a ghost town for very long. The railroad's laid its surveying stakes, and the owner of the town, a lady named Susan Donner, is giving the place away."

"Giving it away? What's in it for her?"

"She's running cattle on a ranch south of town, Henry. She gets the market."

"I see . . ." Horner scratched his chin. "A sort of land rush, huh?"

"You could call it that. There's empty hotels and saloons and barns, all sorts of buildings up there with no one home but rats. These folks figure to get something for nothing."

"Should've raised prices," Henry Horner said, but he wasn't being serious; Horner was a fair man. "Who needs that, though? I've got a month's business this last week. Them out front"—he nodded his head—"are going crazy. Same thing across town at Boone's. They're buying anything that's got more'n three legs. My rolling stock's long gone. Sold a few cripples, one with a busted axle, but I couldn't talk the man out of buying it. Said he'd carve his own out of a tree...." Henry shrugged and gave a little snort, amused by the follies of his fellow man.

"I'd like to talk to those people," Justice said.

"Why? You got horses somewhere, Ruffin?"

"No. I've asked the wagon master if some of those people wouldn't be willing to double up, though. I think the ones that have room will be more than willing, especially if they're offered a few dollars."

"Talk to 'em!" Henry said, slapping the arms of his swivel chair. I got nothing much left to sell, and I'm afraid they're going to tear the place apart if I can't satisfy 'em all."

It wasn't easy to get everybody's attention. Henry's harried hostler was trying to wrestle a piece of harness away from a big man in a blue shirt, and there was a lot of shouting going on. Ruff finally got them to quiet down and listen.

"There just aren't any horses left. The ones you see already belong to people who are boarding them. The wagons are mostly gone ..."

"Just who in hell are you?" the man in the blue shirt demanded belligerently.

"My name's Ruff Justice. The army's sent me to guide you through to Deadwater. Now if you'll listen

31

for a minute . . . I've talked to the people out at the wagon camp. Some of them might be willing to share a ride with you." That brought a small stir, and a few people in the back of the crowd made a break for the river. Ruff went on, "If you'll proceed on out there in an orderly way and wait while they hold their meeting, you will very likely find a way to get to Deadwater. Standing around here yelling and fighting isn't going to get you anything at all. The man has no more stock to sell!"

There was a little more conversation and a few questions, but for the most part Ruff's speech seemed to have calmed them down. They started out, men shouldering bags, women leading small kids. Henry Horner stood beside Ruff, watching them go.

"Tell you something, Ruffin."

"What's that?"

"This was nothing."

"I don't get you, Henry."

The stable owner patted at his face with a red kerchief. "Simple. These people have come a long way. Most of them are near broke, taking a last gamble. They got kids and family . . ."

"Yes?"

"When they get to Deadwater, some of 'em are going to be disappointed, aren't they? That town ain't that big. When some of 'em get those free offered barns and buildings and others don't . . . what happens then, Ruffin? Just what's going to happen then?"

4

"Mr. Ruffin Justice?"

The voice was small, faint, and feminine. Ruff turned away from Horner in the direction of the voice. She was small and blond, nicely put together with wide, sad green eyes and a little puckered mouth that was at once a woman's and a child's.

"Yes, miss."

"I heard it—heard it all. You're a kind man."

"Kind? I was just trying to get everything together to make my job easier."

"I don't believe it. You were concerned about them. . . . I saw it in your eyes."

She came nearer, her own eyes wide and searching. Ruff felt Henry Horner's thick hand fall on his shoulder, then heard Horner's chuckle as he turned away and tramped back to his office to count the receipts.

"What can I do for you?"

"I wanted . . . I don't know anyone here. In Bismarck," she answered. Her hands fluttered ineffectually at her sides as her green eyes batted at Justice.

"What?" Ruff asked. She was a charming thing, a

porcelain doll of a girl. She moved closer to him, smelling of lilac soap and youth.

"I need help."

"What kind of help?"

She looked around as if someone might be listening. The stableyard was empty. "I'm one of the settlers, you see . . ." she began.

"Then you'd better get over to the camp."

"But I don't want to ride with anyone. I've heard of a man," she said, lowering her voice. "A man who has horses and a wagon he might sell. A man named Stallings; do you know who he is?"

"Sure." Aaron Stallings was the biggest rancher around. He had gear all right, and horses.

"I have money." She surreptitiously showed Justice a palmful of gold coins, "But I'm afraid I'll be cheated. I don't even know where his ranch is. I was afraid to ask anyone, afraid that the others might beat me down there. Now," she said, "I'm asking you. *Can* you help me?"

Ruff looked the small woman up and down. "You're all alone in this?" he asked.

"I'm alone. I'm afraid to travel with anyone. I have hopes . . . I want to open a dress shop in Deadwater. My folks are dead. This gold is all I got from the sale of their farm."

Ruff frowned, looked at the ground, and answered, "All right. I'll ride down to Stallings's place with you."

He left her there while he borrowed a horse from Henry. It was the mayor's horse, but the mayor was out of town just then.

"Make sure that thing gets back though, Justice. I've got a permit coming up for renewal." Henry laughed, but there was an edge of concern in his voice. A few horses had already been stolen.

Ruff waved a hand and moved off toward the stable, where he saddled the mayor's strapping glossy bay and led it outside. The girl was waiting, hands clasped.

"I was afraid you wouldn't come back," she said.

"Were you? Why?"

"Oh, you know—a crazy girl asking for help."

"I'm back. Let's get on down to Stallings's and see what he's got. How'd you hear about him?"

"Asking around. A nice woman in the bakery told me."

Ruff helped her onto the bay, recovered his spotted horse, and started southward toward the S-bar-S, the Stallings place. Stallings had the most land around simply because he had gotten there first. He had bought some land from the local Arikara Indians, taken some from the Sioux, and held back all comers. The old man wasn't much to look at these days. He needed a cane to get around, and the meat had melted away from his big-boned frame, but you could still see in his eyes what he had been.

The day was softly warm, the cottonwoods along the Missouri gently fluttering in the light northern breeze. The young woman with the green eyes was riding beside Ruff, so close that he could smell that lilac powder above the scent of horse and leather and flowers surrounding them.

"How far is it?" she asked.

"Five miles to the main house," Justice answered.

"So far?"

"Tired?"

"Very tired." She smiled wearily, and Ruff returned her smile.

"We can stop if you want. You can rinse off."

"Thank you. I'd appreciate it. Up there? In the shade," she suggested.

Justice wouldn't mind a little shade himself, nor would the horses mind some water, loosened cinches, and a rest. They veered toward the oak-lined area along the river the girl had indicated. There, a tongue of sandy beach projected into the broad Missouri.

It was shady but warm, larks crowding the trees. Ruff's horse blew once and tossed its head. They swung down on a gravelly beach littered with driftwood. The girl stretched out her arms for Ruff's help, slid down, and went to the river's edge to dab at her face and neck with a small white handkerchief.

She glanced back at him once, then again. Justice couldn't make out her expression.

"Come to me," she said, and then he saw that she had opened the first three buttons of her dress to pat at her breasts with the cloth. "Come here, Mr. Justice."

He came nearer, watching her breasts rise and fall with her breathing, hearing the wind sing in the old oaks, seeing the glitter of the wide Missouri behind her.

And then he saw it in her eyes.

Later he couldn't be sure if it was shadows from her soul, a trick of perception, or the actual image as he drew close enough to make mirrors of her eyes.

But he saw him. Justice saw the gunman in black and threw himself to the ground, rolling over as the Remington pistol spat flame, kicking dirt and gravel into Ruff's face.

As he rolled, Justice reached for and found his Colt, his thumb hooking back the hammer as naturally as taking a breath. He came to one knee, his long, dark hair hanging in his face, squeezed the curved trigger of the pistol, and scored with his first bullet.

He saw the fabric of the man in black's shirt leap, saw the blood spew from his lips, saw him stagger back, dropping one Remington and grabbing for the second, holstered one.

Justice distantly heard the woman's scream, saw her fingers go to her mouth, her green eyes open wider. But his attention was on the gunman, only on the man in black.

Justice came to his feet as the man cleared leather with his left-hand gun. Ruff stood, dueling fashion, his arm fully extended, and fired again. His arm leapt as black powder smoke briefly flooded the clearing before the wind whipped it away.

The bullet stopped the man in black's heart. It hit dead center, and the left-hand gun never got up. The spinning .44 from Ruff's Colt's barrel slammed the gunman back against the earth where he lay, one knee raised, twitching for a minute.

Ruff shifted his sights briefly to the girl, who stood pale and rigid, watching. Then, holstering the Colt, he walked to the body.

He hadn't seen the man before. Tall, dark, dressed in black. He had the trigger guards cut off his engraved Remington pistols. The guns had notches cut into their grips.

Ruff kicked the left-hand gun aside and crouched, searching the body. He found three hundred dollars in gold in a money belt, and a playing card in the breast pocket of his coat.

The jack of diamonds. There was a .44 caliber hole through the face of the jack. Ruff pocketed the card and stood, slowly surveying the trees, wondering if this gunman was the only one.

Assuring himself that the man in black had been alone, Ruff returned to the spotted pony, snatching up his crumpled hat.

"What are you doing? What happened . . . ?" the girl asked.

Justice took the reins to the bay horse and started off, leaving the girl behind. .

"Wait!" she cried out. "Why are you leaving me? What am I supposed to do? How do I get back to town?"

Ruff reined up and half turned in the saddle. Fishing in his pocket, he flipped the girl one of the gold coins, noticing its crimson stain.

"Buy a horse from Stallings."

"But I had nothing to do with this!" She leaned toward him, her hands clutching at the air. "Nothing!"

"That bakery where the nice woman told you about the Stallings place . . . it burned down last week."

Justice turned his horse and rode out, leaving the woman shrieking and cursing at his back. As he rode he thought about the man in black, trying to place him, wondering why he had that single card on his body. But Ruff had other things to put his mind to—the wagon train. He wondered how McCulloch had done in the election for wagon master.

"McCulloch," Ruff said with a tight little smile. He hadn't liked those saloon girls at all. "The man should learn to trust women," Justice said dryly. Then he tugged his hat lower, and with a single glance back toward the oak grove, rode on toward Bismarck and the wagon camp beyond.

McCulloch was wagon master.

"No one else," Ortega told him, "seemed to want the job. Too much aggravation, no pay."

"McCulloch's suited. He wants the authority. Where is he?"

Ortega lifted a pointing finger. Then he frowned at Justice and asked, "You hurt? There's blood on your shirt, hombre."

Ruff glanced down. "Just a little dirt, I guess."

"Sure," Ortega said. "Me, I've seen enough of that kind of dirt in my time."

Justice found McCulloch with two men in city suits. One of them was the gambler, Tibbits. McCulloch's expression was obstinate.

Justice waited until they were through with their conference and then swung down.

"Well, you fixed us, Justice. Sent a plague of locusts our way."

"It seemed like the thing to do."

"The thing to do! A couple of people got turned away, and they got real nasty. Threatened to get even."

"A big man in a blue shirt," Ruff guessed.

McCulloch blinked, "Why, yes, he was one of them. Tibbits and that crony of his wanted to know what we're going to do to protect ourselves."

"Tibbits is the one who turned the man down."

"One of them—everybody turned that big bastard down. Christ, what a hothead. You'd think we were heading for the goldfields."

"What are you going to do about protection?" Ruff Justice asked.

"Do? That's the army's job, isn't it?"

"My job, you mean."

"That's right. If these latecomers are going to try anything, I figure it's your job to stop them."

"All right." Justice didn't know exactly how he was going to go about it, but he also figured that whatever

39

threats had been made came out of a moment's frustration, temporary anger.

He was dead wrong.

Dusk was beginning to settle. It had been a short but eventful day. There was much about it that disturbed him. He told McCulloch, "I'd like you to ask around for a few men willing to stand watch tonight."

"I'll do that," McCulloch said. "But this is still your job. This man Court—Dan Court—the one you're talking about. He's mad, Justice, mad clean through. He smells profit, and he wants some of it. I've heard a few stories about him. I don't think he's above trying to wreck this wagon train if it means him and his people can get through to Deadwater first."

"Maybe not. We'll see. Find a few men and send them to me, will you?"

"Sure. Damned army . . ." McCulloch muttered. "Could've sent more'n one scout along with us. Anything could happen. Anything at all."

"We'll try to see it doesn't. You might try Ortega—he seems to be a man who knows what's going on. A few of the cowboys as well. At least they know which end of a gun is which."

"The greaser and the cowboys, I got you," McCulloch said. He was tired of talking. "Where can they find you?"

"I'll be right here. But first I want to talk to a lady."

"One of them . . . ?"

"Mary Caffiter."

"Mary Caffiter, is it. She told some people about you, Justice—told them you'd gunned her son down. I don't think she'll want to talk to you again, do you?"

"No, but she's going to," Justice answered. "She's going to talk, and she's going to listen."

And maybe she would do a little explaining.

The man in black was still foremost in Ruff's mind—the man in black with the cut-down guns. A hired killer, no doubt about it. A man who lived for his guns, who prided himself on them and what they had done.

The name came back slowly to Justice—a face he'd once seen on a wanted poster: Jud Hollister. He was a Kansas gun originally, drifting out of that state to avoid a murder charge. He had drifted from a good many others for the same reason. He was reputed to have been good, and to be expensive.

His fee was at least three hundred dollars in gold. Someone nearby must have paid him that kind of money to eliminate Ruffin T. Justice.

Sundown was a burst of orange and violet light through the dark columns of the oaks. The river was colored as deeply as the sky, slowly flowing southward. Beyond the trees Bismarck sparkled dully as the lanterns were lit and the nightlife began.

Mary Caffiter was sitting on the tailgate of her wagon, sewing a button on a faded dress. She had removed her bonnet, and her head looked nearly skull-like, ancient and frail. Her eyes lifted to meet Justice's.

"You go away," she said.

"Can't do that," Justice said, propping a foot up on the rear wheel of the wagon and removing his hat to wipe back his long, dark hair. "We have to talk."

"What's there to talk about?"

"This." Ruff's finger held a small, thin object. He held it up to her.

"What's that?"

"The jack of diamonds, I think." Justice poked his finger through the .44 caliber hole in the bloodstained card.

"I see that, Mr. Justice," the old woman said sharply. "You know what I mean—why show it to me?"

"I thought maybe you'd seen it before."

"I don't play cards."

"No? Billy Lane did," Ruff told her. "Billy Lane Caffiter played cards, and when he lost he got mad, and when he got mad he killed people."

"They say!"

"They say the truth," Ruff Justice said honestly. Billy Lane had been a cruel, vicious little thug with an eagerness to kill. The only thing Justice regretted was that he hadn't killed him earlier, before Billy had gunned down a woman on the streets of Newton, Kansas and an unarmed sodbuster in North Platte.

His mother just sat there, shaking her head, her fingers too unsteady to sew any longer.

"What do you want?" she asked finally.

"To know if you're trying to have me killed."

Her head lifted; tears streamed down her sunken cheeks. "If I knew how to go about it, I would. If I thought that my killing you would bring Billy Lane back to life, I would. You don't deserve to live, Justice."

"Probably not," Justice commented quietly.

Who did deserve to live? Killers and congressmen and cowboys and soldiers and the rich and the poor—all just wasting their lives, doing little to help when help was needed. Maybe no one deserved to have life; but certainly no one deserved to be gunned down in his prime.

The woman was sewing angrily, violently, when Ruff Justice turned on his heel and walked away across the dusk-darkened wagon camp.

It was hard to believe Billy Lane's mother had hired

Jud Hollister, but then Justice had always been a sucker for the ladies—especially frail old ones or young helpless ones.

"Where would she have gotten the money?" he asked himself. Where indeed. Three hundred dollars was a year's wages in most jobs; saving up an amount like that was no mean task.

But if not Mary Caffiter, who? Who hated Justice that much, enough to have him gunned down by a professional like Jud Hollister?

Justice smiled slowly, grimly. He could think of quite a few who would have done it for nothing.

"Justice!"

It was Felipe Ortega, coming on the run, his rifle in hand. He was shouting something, but Ruff couldn't hear him. Then the sudden thunder of guns beyond the camp began a fiery crescendo, and the death angels began to scream in the bloody night.

5

"Justice!" Ortega panted. He gripped the tall man's shoulder and pointed to the west. "They're hitting us."

"Who? Dan Court?"

"I don't know. Come on . . . too many guns."

Then Justice was running beside Ortega toward the far side of the camp. The guns had blared; smoke filled the camp, but now it was suddenly silent. Justice knew somehow that the attackers had already made a hasty retreat.

They found McCulloch there along with a few cowboys. The gambler, Tibbits, stood with his rifle in his hands, proving that the long nights in saloons and gambling halls had left him with a firm grasp of American cussing.

"What happened?" Ruff asked.

"Where the hell were you?" McCulloch demanded.

"Are you going to tell me or not?"

Tibbits told him. "Bastards hit us hard. Guns everywhere. You can see what happened."

He lifted a lantern, and Justice could see what had happened all right. Six horses were dead on the ground, and one ox was still struggling to rise, its hoofs thrashing.

"Killed the stock."

"What in God's name did that gain 'em? Why do something like this?"

"Revenge," Justice said. He walked to the still-kicking ox, placed the muzzle of his Colt behind its ear, and touched off. The report was loud in the night. The ox lay motionless beside the other dead animals.

"I'm not standing for this," McCulloch said. "I'm going to get the marshal."

"Think it over," Ruff cautioned him.

"Think it over? The bastard killed our stock!"

"Did anyone see them? Can anyone identify them?" Justice asked.

"We know damn well who it was," Tibbits insisted.

"Try taking that to court."

"I'm not letting Dan Court get away with this," the wagon master said. He turned and lifted his arms like a politician trying to spur his people on.

"In the first place," Ruff Justice said, "you don't know for sure that it was Dan Court. The marshal's going to have to have some proof before he could do a damn thing about it."

"We'll get proof."

"Fine," Justice went on, "and then what? You want to stay around Bismarck while they get up a jury, wait for the circuit judge, and have a trial? That'll take months, weeks, anyway. Meanwhile all the others are going to be beating you to Deadwater."

"We can't let him get away with it," Tibbits shouted.

"You can't prosecute, either. If you did and you won, you'd all just lose what you came to Bismarck for: a chance at a life in Deadwater. Besides that, what do you think the penalty's going to be if they find Dan Court guilty of shooting some horses and an ox? Think they're going to string him up for that? Not likely, boys."

"He's liable to strike again, and the next time it might not be horses and an ox."

"Maybe not. We'll have to chance that. Let's get organized and protect ourselves."

"And what's the army doing for us?" McCulloch asked.

"The best they can, I suppose," Ruff Justice said.

"You?"

"Me."

The following silence was a healthy comment on what they thought about that statement. There wasn't much to say or do but try to organize a guard and get the dead stock buried. Some of their wagons were going to be heavily overloaded now, and Justice knew what McCulloch was thinking. If Justice hadn't sent those people out from town to find a ride to share, none of this would have happened.

Maybe not. You make a choice and do it. You're lucky if you're right fifty percent of the time.

"Ortega?"

"Yes, Justice."

"Find us some good men. We need soldiers, and we're probably going to need them for a long time—all the way to Deadwater."

It was nearly midnight before they had gotten anything accomplished. The married men were wary about taking up guns and going out into the night. A few of the single men were equally wary, maybe more so. For the most part these people were merchants, townsmen, storekeepers. They didn't much relish running into a band of armed men.

Ruff found a handful, however; a few men who would do the job—or so he hoped.

Ortega was first on his list—the Mexican hostler had seen fighting somewhere, sometime. He might not have liked it, but he was willing to do it to protect himself.

Three cowboys up from Texas, led by a long-limbed, languid man named Beers, who wore chaps and crossed six-guns, volunteered. "I been sleepin' too much anyway lately," Beers said, yawning. He asked Ruff, "This lady cattle rancher out at Dead-water. She one of these hard cases, all thorns and bristles?"

"Susan Donner. No. She's young and decent and looks like a puff of wind would break her. It won't. She's got strength when she needs it. She'll do right by you boys."

"Glad to hear it," Beers said. "We've rid a long ways. Took a herd through to Kansas, got rousted, got in a fight with the cheatin' trail boss, kept ridin'."

He didn't say it, but Justice had the idea the cheatin' trail boss hadn't ridden on. Anywhere.

Ruff got his men posted and then spent some time alone near the river, thinking. He thought about Susan Donner and how he was going to tell her that Mike had been killed by the Indians. Then he thought about Mary Caffiter and the anger she was carrying; and about Dan Court, who was carrying his own anger to a dangerous length.

He thought about that jack of diamonds.

The river flowed coldly past in the night, and Justice watched it for a while, fingering the piece of pasteboard he was carrying.

Thinking and wondering. . . .

*   *   *

"Where's the old woman got to?" Wiley Pabst demanded. He was half-drunk, his red eyes dull and glassy. The Apache lifted his head slowly from the game of solitaire he had spread out before him on the green table.

"Gone."

"Gone? Gone where?"

"Said she was going along."

Pabst shook his head. Nothing much was clear in his mind right now. He had spent a third of his pay gambling and drinking in Bismarck. The Apache, blue-eyed and savage, watched him.

"Gone on ahead." The Apache shrugged. "Wanted to keep an eye on Justice."

"That don't make no sense—what about Jud Hollister? She'll just be in his way."

The Apache didn't answer. He nodded toward the table in the corner. Two Remington pistols, engraved, with the trigger guards cut away, rested there.

"The son of a bitch got Hollister!" Wiley Pabst breathed.

The Apache didn't answer. He had risen like a cat and moved to the open cabin door. The bastard was too quiet. Wiley hadn't even been aware of his movement. It was unnerving.

"The old woman left. What are we supposed to do now?"

Framed in the doorway, backlighted by stars winking through the oaks along the river, the Apache turned and walked back to the table. He stacked the deck of cards and gestured for Wiley to cut.

"High card?" Wiley asked.

The Apache nodded, and Wiley Pabst cut a queen out of the deck. The Apache frowned, cut himself, and turned up a seven of spades.

"It's yours," the Apache said.

Then he sat down and began dealing a hand of solitaire.

"He's mine, all right," Pabst said. The other seven hundred in gold was going to be his. He went outside, trying to clear his alcohol-fogged mind. The river was dark and cold. Wiley Pabst walked from the boat, listening to the infernal clamor of frogs and crickets. He crouched down at the river's edge and dipped his head under water, feeling the bite of the cold.

When he lifted his whiskered face, he felt better. He sat back on his haunches, rolling a cigarette. Ruff Justice.

He had gotten Jud Hollister—it didn't seem possible, but he had. Was Justice that fast?

Wiley lit his cigarette and tossed the match into the river, where it hissed into extinction.

Jud Hollister was the fastest man Wiley had ever seen. It didn't seem likely that some army scout, no matter how tough he was supposed to be, could outdraw Hollister. He just couldn't have spent the time practicing that Hollister had. Pabst had seen Hollister spend three hours a day, day after day: drawing, firing, drawing, firing.

He didn't get him that way, not in a stand-up fight, Pabst decided. *Maybe Jud tried to get too cute about it. Probably tried to set him up with some scheme that went wrong. Got himself blown up.*

That wasn't Pabst's way of doing things. You shot the man and he died. That was the only plan Wiley Pabst had ever utilized. And it had always worked just as well as anything else. He shot them; they died.

He walked to where he had left his horse, saddled up, and shoved the cold steel bit into the reluctant sorrel's mouth. Striding back to the flatboat, he entered the cabin where the Apache sat in the same position, playing solitaire.

"I'm going now," Pabst said. The Apache nodded. "I'm going to join up with that wagon train. Justice don't know me. I'll get close to the bastard somehow or another."

The Apache lifted his blue eyes and shrugged. If it wasn't his work, he didn't need to know about it. He had three hundred dollars and a place to stay out of the weather. He had no interest in the bulky, ripely scented Wiley Pabst or his plan.

Pabst snatched up his burlap sack full of supplies, scowled at the Apache, and went out, banging the door behind him.

His sorrel was waiting, and Pabst swung aboard.

"Maybe tonight," Pabst told himself. "Maybe I can take him tonight and save everybody a lot of trouble."

Then he could get back to his drinking and that card game down at the Golden Spur Saloon. He glanced back and saw the Apache standing in the doorway, watching. He started to lift his hand in farewell but gave up the idea. He heeled his sorrel forward, aiming toward the wagon camp to the north where he could already see the soft glow of many campfires like beacons in the night.

Summoning death.

Wiley didn't like the setup when he arrived. They had armed guards out, and that was sure to put the clamps on any escape. It looked like the card game was out for tonight. There was another thing Pabst couldn't quite figure. A body of men, separate from the wagon train, was camped a mile or so south. They had no fires, which bothered Wiley, since it was a cold night. Who the hell were they?

"Halt!" someone called out sharply, and Wiley

nearly went for his gun. It was a good thing he didn't. The Mexican was half-hidden behind a tree, rifle ready and leveled at Pabst.

"What the hell's the matter?" Pabst demanded.

"Who are you and what do you want?"

"Will Handy." The name came easily to Pabst's lips. He had used the name a number of times in a number of places when he was laying low. The Mexican came forward a little, and Pabst raised his hands higher.

"All right, Will Handy," Ortega said, "what do you want here?"

"For Christ's sake—ain't this the wagon train heading for Deadwater? I just come out to ride along," Pabst complained. "What's the matter with you people?"

"We've had some trouble," Ortega said. He was eyeing Pabst closely. There was something familiar about him.

"Well, I don't know about that. I've come along peaceful, wanting some company to Deadwater. How about lowering the rifle."

"Just ride on ahead, slowly," Ortega said. "I'm coming right behind you."

"Sure," Pabst said, trying for a smile. A smile, he had found, loosened people up quickly. You smiled and then when you saw them relax, you shot them. But Wiley Pabst had no intention of shooting the Mexican. He had another target in mind. He did his best to become amiable Will Handy.

"You scared hell out of me jumping out from behind that tree. Someone give you folks a bad time?"

"Someone did, yes," Ortega snswered. He walked behind the sorrel as they entered the camp. His rifle hadn't lowered a notch. There was something about this one. . . .

They found Ruff Justice at a campfire with two other men, both cowboys, judging from their dress. Ruff rose, coffee cup in hand, and Wiley Pabst got a first look at his victim—the man who had somehow killed Jud Hollister.

Ruff Justice was tall and lean, and there was knowledge in his eyes. He wore buckskins and a wide-brimmed white hat with what looked like a lady's red scarf tied around it. Yes, he was tough enough.

But not tough enough to beat a bullet in his heart. Wiley Pabst smiled and swung down.

"Everyone's a little jittery, it seems. What's up?"

Justice told him. "A few men wanted to come along. There wasn't any room, and they started a fight. Killed some stock."

"I seen 'em," Pabst said. Why not tell Justice? Put himself on the right side. "About a mile south. Half a dozen men in a cold camp."

McCulloch had strolled up to the fire to listen. He wore a bulky mackintosh faded blue and yellow. The wagon master wanted some action.

"Let's get down there and clean 'em out."

"Settle down," Justice said. "We don't need any vigilante work."

"Scared?"

Justice was silent for a long moment. Finally he answered, "You go out there, and someone's going to get killed. Maybe you. Maybe one of them—if that happens, you're a killer."

"What are we supposed to do, let Dan Court get away with this?"

"Court will likely get over it soon. He's worked off some frustration. You forget they haven't got any horses. As soon as we pull out, they'll be left behind."

"So you say," McCulloch said sourly.

"So I hope. What I know is that a raid on those men is more trouble than you want, more than it's worth. Leave 'em be."

Wiley Pabst saw the tall man toss the dregs of his coffee into the fire and pick up a sheathed buffalo gun. He nodded to Ortega.

"I'll stand watch for a while. Where's Beers?"

"Along the river."

"Send someone along to relieve him around midnight."

"All right, Justice."

Ruff looked again at McCulloch and then at the new man. This new man was watching him with an expression Justice didn't quite get. Was it possible that Dan Court had sent him over? *No-damn it,* Justice thought, *I'm getting jumpy over nothing, over the softest assignment I've had in a long while. Take the wagons through, leave Dan Court behind to sulk, and get back home as soon as possible.*

He nodded again and walked off into the night, feeling those eyes on his back.

"He's wrong," the man called Will Handy said to McCulloch.

"Damn right . . . what'd you say your name was?"

Handy introduced himself. The two men shook hands, and Wiley Pabst prodded the wagon master again. "I think he's scared."

"I don't know about that, but he's sure as hell thinking wrong about this. Go down and drive those men off, I say. That's the way I'd handle it. This Justice, he does things his own way. No matter if I'm wagon boss or not."

"Maybe," Wiley Pabst said ambiguously, "something ought to be done about him."

McCulloch's eyes flashed. Then he smiled and said,

"Maybe so. Come on over and have some coffee, Handy. If that's not to your taste, I got something that comes in a bottle that'll warm your ears for you."

For a moment longer Wiley Pabst watched the dark woods where Ruff Justice had disappeared. Then he turned back to McCulloch.

"Sure," he said with his Will Handy smile. "Let's have us a drink and some talk."

It never hurt to have friends, Pabst thought. He might have some use for this bullheaded wagon master. "Let's just have ourselves a small drink."

6

They rolled out with the red light of dawn behind them. A long line of jolting, creaking wagons, heavily overloaded, stretched out toward the west, toward Deadwater and hope.

Beers caught up with Justice as he waited at a ford, watching the inexperienced wagoneers try to make their crossing.

"Someone to see you," the Texan said.

"Who?"

"The law, it seems like. I came ahead"—Beers grinned—"figuring to tell you in case you were wanted."

"Not me," Justice answered. "Not that I know of." He added, "Maybe you ought to lay low, though." There was still that trail boss in Kansas.

Beers grinned. "That's the other reason I came on ahead. He's back there talking to McCulloch. Red-headed man wearing a town marshal's badge."

"That'll be Sturges out of Bismarck. I'd better see what he wants." Ruff gestured toward the river—it was narrow but quick, shallow but muddy. "I'd appreciate it if you'd watch the ford. Some of these people got no idea what they're doing."

"Sure thing. . . . When you find out what the marshal wants . . ."

"I'll let you know, Beers," Ruff promised.

Justice turned the spotted horse back, riding past the long line of would-be settlers. There were far too many of them, he thought. What *would* happen when some of them found nothing in Deadwater?

"Hello, handsome!" a woman's voice called out, and Ruff lifted his eyes to the wagon where the three saloon girls had been given a ride. They were sitting on the tailgate and had changed from their flashy clothes into cotton and gingham. The redheaded one waved and blew a kiss his way. "Come back and see us now, Mister Scout!"

"I just might," he called.

"You make that a promise, tall man."

Ruff laughed and waved and went on, his thoughts growing serious again. Had McCulloch gone into Bismarck for Sturges, or did the marshal have something else on his mind? Sturges hated to leave his desk; if he was here, it could only mean more trouble of one kind or another.

He found the marshal riding on the bench seat of McCulloch's wagon, leading his horse, which walked along beside them, head down.

"Howdy, Sturges!"

"Justice!" The marshal lifted a hand.

"What's the trouble?" Ruff asked, turning his horse.

"I'll tell you what the trouble is," McCulloch began hotly.

The marshal interrupted him. "Nothing much, I don't suppose. . . ."

"Nothing!" McCulloch was fuming.

"Go ahead, Sturges," Justice said.

"Last night some boys broke into the Horner Brothers stable and stole a bunch of stock, including the mayor's bay. There were some mighty angry men in town this morning when they went to reclaim their horses."

"It was Dan Court," McCulloch said positively.

"Maybe," Sturges said thoughtfully. He told Ruff Justice, "The wagon master here's been telling me about the little run-in you had with this Dan Court. Think it was them?"

"Wouldn't doubt it a bit," Justice said.

"Well, keep your eyes open. Main reason I came out was to see if someone in this train had those horses, but I can see they aren't here."

McCulloch said, "We can track them down."

"Maybe. Me, I'm *town* marshal. We're a good ways from Bismarck already. You don't know what it's like to try finding someone on these plains. But don't worry, we'll find 'em. I'll get descriptions of those horses off to all the neighboring towns. They'll show up—and when they do"—he shrugged—"somebody'll hang the thieves."

"And what if Court attacks us? You didn't tell Justice what you knew about Court."

"No, I didn't." Sturges explained, "I've seen Court's name before. He used to be some kind of guerilla raider down in Missouri. He's a pretty brutal fellow. Whether he would come back after the wagon train for revenge or just to see what he could get out of it, I don't know. . . . Tell you this, if you do see him, don't mess with him. There's a dead-or-alive poster out on him. You know what I'm telling you, Justice."

"Yeah, Sturges, I know."

He was telling Ruff Justice that if he got the chance he should gun Dan Court down and do Sturges's job for him. "Anything else?" Ruff wanted to know.

"Nothing. You people take care." Sturges rose, stepped onto his horse's saddle, and pulled away from the wagon train.

"Bastard—what's he do to earn his pay?" McCulloch muttered.

"All he can, I guess," Justice answered.

"And just what are we supposed to do?"

"Keep our eyes open."

"This is your fault, Justice. You know that, don't you? You brought Court out to us. You wouldn't let us go down there last night and stamp the vermin out."

"I don't think it's anybody's fault. Listen, McCulloch, my one and only concern is to get everyone through to Deadwater. That's what Colonel MacEnroe sent me out here to do. I brought some extra people along to help *them* get there. I tried to talk you out of attacking Court's camp to make sure *you* got there. Now all I can do is see that Court doesn't give us any more trouble."

"By riding patrol," McCulloch scoffed.

"That's right."

"I would've made sure he didn't give us any trouble. . . ." McCulloch said, staring sullenly ahead over the backs of his horses.

There wasn't much point in continuing this conversation, Ruff figured, so he veered away, still hearing McCulloch's grumbling complaints.

"What's the matter with our scout?"

McCulloch turned his head to the other side of the wagon. The man he knew as Will Handy was riding beside him on his tall sorrel.

"I don't know. Scared? You tell me."

"I think he just wants to be boss. And," Wiley Pabst said, "I think he's dead wrong. You had the right idea last night about how to handle someone like this Court."

"Well, thanks, Handy, you seem to be the only one who thinks so."

"You also got good whisky," Wiley Pabst said, and McCulloch laughed.

"Swing aboard. There's a jug in the back. I wouldn't mind washing my throat a little."

Pabst did that, mounting over the tailgate while the wagon was on the move and tethering the sorrel to the back. He found the jug, and ducked through to the seat, where he planted himself beside McCulloch.

"Bastard," McCulloch said after a long pull from the jug. It wasn't evident whether he meant Dan Court or Ruff Justice. Wiley Pabst decided to press the issue.

"There's one way to get rid of rattlesnakes that I know of.

"Just one way. . . ." McCulloch glanced at Wiley Pabst, and for a moment he was puzzled by something in the man's eyes. Another pull on the jug wiped away his uncertainty. Will Handy was his friend, maybe the only man he could really trust. They thought alike.

"Have another drink, Handy," McCulloch said, and Wiley Pabst obliged. For a while the men sat side by side on the sun-heated wagon, eating dust from the teams ahead and thinking quiet, sullen thoughts.

Ruff Justice had long since quit thinking about McCulloch; he wasn't worth the wasted effort. Ruff had drifted away from the wagon train toward the south. The air was cool and clean and the grass long. The prairie rolled away gently in all directions. Scattered fleecy clouds moved across the deep blue sky.

Ruff was looking for tracks. It figured Court would

be to the south of the slow-moving wagon train, heading for Deadwater.

McCulloch was convinced that Court was going to raid the wagon train—maybe so—but it was also possible that Court would simply take his men and beeline it for the empty town, laying claim to the choice pieces of property. These could be sold to the newcomers or to other interests.

It was all speculation, but it was worth thinking about. When Justice did find the tracks, it surprised him. One horse. One rider crossing the plains in the direction of the Flame River and Deadwater beyond.

The tracks might have nothing at all to do with the rest of the trouble, but then again maybe they did.

Justice frowned. The wind was brisker now, shifting his horse's mane and causing the fringes on his buckskin shirt to flutter and drift.

The rifle report crackled across the prairie, and Justice dove for the ground as the spotted horse, tagged high on the neck, reared up and danced away.

Justice had the sheath off his big .56 Spencer and now, flat on the ground, his eyes combed the distances ahead of him. He could still see a tiny puff of smoke nearly five hundred yards away. Whoever was shooting had an eye.

There was no second shot. Ruff watched the knolls which lifted from the flat prairie, but he could see nothing. It seemed hours later when he heard hoofbeats and saw the tiny figure of a horse being ridden away. There wasn't even any point in trying an answering shot.

Justice rose, brushed himself off, and walked the quarter mile to where the spotted horse stood watching him accusingly. These man-games, the horse's eyes seemed to say, are painful.

It wasn't much more than a nick that the horse had taken, a long shallow crease along the side of its neck. Painful, but not dangerous.

Ruff swung aboard. The horse balked a little, reluctant to continue, but Justice got it settled and pointed it toward the place where he had seen smoke.

He found the spot after another hour's searching. The horse's tracks there were the same as those he had seen earlier. Ruff found the single .44-40 cartridge gleaming dully against the grass. He picked it up, smelled it, and dropped it again.

Something else had caught his eye. A fragment of material, no more than a few snagged black threads. Ruff crouched and picked them up from the grass.

It was difficult to tell for sure what they had been torn from, but they looked for all the world like a part of a lady's lace gloves—the kind the older women wore when they were in mourning or were on their way to church.

"And what the hell sense does that make?"

None that Ruff could put a handle on. He swung aboard the spotted pony again and began cautiously trailing the sniper's horse. On the far side of the knoll a narrow silver creek snaked its way across the land. The sniper had ridden into it and turned—north or south?

Ruff tried north, riding half a mile or so upstream as the wind grew colder, but he found no more tracks, no place where the rider could have emerged from the stream.

He could turn and ride south, but the sniper was long gone now, and it was time to get back to the wagon camp. They would need help finding a place to set up for the night, and Justice was wasting his time out here.

He took a deep breath and let it out angrily. He didn't like being shot at. He especially didn't like it when he didn't even know what it was all about.

It had to be one of Court's people, didn't it? But then how could you explain the threads? Some kind of fancy black shirt?

Ruff shook his head, wheeled the spotted pony, and pointed it up the knoll to his right, heading back toward the wagon train.

He could see that the oxen and horses were settled into their yokes and harnesses now, plodding on toward some unknown destination, wading wearily through the long sea of grass.

Justice found McCulloch alone on his wagon bench.

"There's water just over the rise," Justice said. "It might be a good idea to circle up on that knoll and water the stock."

"There's plenty of daylight left," McCulloch said stubbornly.

"Plenty of daylight, but if you wait until dusk, you're going to be trying to set up camp in the dark."

McCulloch just nodded, and Justice turned his horse away angrily. It had been a long day, and he wasn't in the mood for the wagon master.

An hour later the wagons had more or less gathered up on the knoll. Two women had started their cooking fires, using buffalo chips, which were plentiful, for fuel.

Justice led his own horse to water again and stood watching it drink. It was there that the trouble began. He didn't see the start of it, but he heard it. A shriek, a catlike hiss, and then a chorus of shouting voices. He looked upstream in time to see the two women clash.

The redhead, her skirts hiked up, leapt at the stocky, bonneted figure, yanking at her hair, kicking and scratching. The two of them toppled over into the stream as several other women and laughing men came running.

Justice started in that direction as a stream of unladylike curses spilled from the lips of the stocky woman.

"Redheaded whore . . ." the shout turned into a choked sputtering as her opponent ducked her head under water. Justice recognized the redhead—one of the painted ladies McCulloch was so upset about.

The other woman's head came up. Gasping, she shouted again, "Whore, trying to seduce my husband . . ." The head was ducked under water again.

McCulloch was coming on the run, and Justice figured it was time to break this up—before McCulloch did it his way. He waded out, took the redhead by the belt, and lifted her, clawing and wriggling, off the settler woman.

The stocky woman sat up in the water, dazed and furious. "Kill her . . . I swear it . . ."

Justice turned his back and took the snarling, clawing captive to the shore, where he plunked her down.

"Damn you!" the redhead said. "What'd you break it up for? I'll claw her eyes out."

"Just take it easy. You won."

"She can't call me what she called me. I can't help it if her damned sodbuster husband gawks when I walk by."

McCulloch was in a rage. He took Justice by the shoulder and tried to pull him aside. Justice slapped his hand away and turned on him.

"It's under control, McCulloch."

"The hell it is! You take *her* side, do you? I knew these women would be trouble."

"Take it easy. It's done with. No harm done."

McCulloch couldn't leave well enough alone. "They're trouble—and so are you. Every bit of this is your fault, Justice. Every piece of bad luck we've had, you brought on."

Then McCulloch made his biggest mistake of the day. His big fists were bunched at his sides, and now the right hooked up, whipping through the air toward Ruff's skull.

Justice pulled away from the right, but a following left tagged him on the neck below his ear, and there wasn't much he could do then but take it to the big man.

Justice took it to him.

7

Justice took the left hook to the neck, ducked away, and staggered a little. McCulloch was a big man, and he could hit hard. The wagon master wanted to finish it quickly. He moved in, trying to drive Justice into the ground with a windmilling overhand right. Justice blocked him with his forearm and drove his own right into McCulloch's belly.

The big man grunted and took a half step back. Justice came upright as he did so and shot a straight left into the wagon master's face. Blood spewed from McCulloch's nose, and he backed off, pawing at his face.

Justice missed with a left, dug a right into McCulloch's ribs, and took a hard right to the top of his skull. He could see movement around him, see the crowd gathering, hear the hoots and whistles and shouts of encouragement.

The sun was dropping rapidly; a purple blur against the eastern sky was all that remained of the day. Justice circled as McCulloch tried to come in on him, his face a furious, bloody mask.

McCulloch kicked at Ruff's kneecap and missed,

tried another overhand right and muttered, "Bastard. You bastard, Justice. I'll kill you with my bare hands."

He stormed in, trying to do just that, but he had failed to protect his chin. Justice winged a right toward that target and caught the big man flush.

McCulloch staggered back and fell into the creek. He rose with a roar, grabbing for Ruff, catching the front of his shirt, yanking him forward. Both men went down into the icy water.

The current was quick. The cold bit at Justice's flesh as water flooded his nostrils. McCulloch was no boxer, but he had his hands on Justice now, and he was bull-strong and determined.

The wagon master got his hands on Ruff's throat, and his thick thumbs dug into Ruff's flesh. Justice got his arms inside McCulloch's and drove them up and out, breaking the hold.

McCulloch kicked out savagely as Justice tried to get to his feet. His boot toe caught Justice on the thigh, deadening it, and Ruff staggered.

McCulloch was on his feet again, water dripping from his sodden clothes and washing his hair into his eyes. He looked like some mad water creature, risen from the depths. Then he came in again.

He clutched at Ruff, missed, and took a right to the wind for his trouble. Half doubling up, McCulloch backed away temporarily, but he wasn't finished. He began winging punches from every direction. Justice took one on his shoulder, had another graze his jaw.

But McCulloch was still carrying his hands low, and his punches were no longer fast. Ruff began to pick him apart.

A left stabbed out and smashed the wagon master's already damaged nose. As McCulloch tried to cover his face, Ruff whistled a solid right to the heart, and

McCulloch staggered. Boring in, Justice feinted with a left and winged in another right-hand shot, this one to the belly. McCulloch's hands dropped automatically, and Justice finished him.

The left-hand hook came up and tagged McCulloch's ear. Blood wormed down his cheek. The right which followed was the one Justice wanted, the one he had been trying to set up. His hooking fist caught the wagon master on the hinge of the jaw, and it was a good one. Ruff could feel the jolt of it down his arm and spine all the way to his toes.

McCulloch's eyes rolled back, and he went out, flopping back into the stream, and forming a dark island in the water.

Panting, Justice went to him and yanked his inert body upright—it wouldn't do anyone any good to let McCulloch drown.

He dragged him to the shore and let him drop there to lie groaning, his unseeing eyes rolling open. Then Ruff heard the sound of the Winchester being cocked and his hand went for his Colt. But the pistol was gone, lost somehow in the fight, and he could only turn slowly to watch as the new man, Will Handy, shouldered his rifle and sighted at Justice's head.

"That's a bad idea, mister," Felipe Ortega said. "It was a fair fight, not a killing matter." Ortega held a scattergun in his hands, its twin muzzles like railroad tunnels trained on Will Handy.

"It's not a killing matter," another man agreed. It was the gambler, Tibbits. "Christ. They lost their tempers and had a fistfight. It's over. Why don't both of you put those damned guns down?"

"Him first," Ortega said, and slowly Will Handy lowered his rifle.

Justice saw it then, the determination in Handy's

eyes. He wanted to shoot, to kill. Why? Was he that great a friend of McCulloch's? They had only just met. Ruff frowned. He watched, waiting until Handy had lowered his rifle, turned, and walked away.

Justice let out a slow breath. "Thanks, Ortega."

"*Por nada*. We need our scout, eh?"

"Some people don't seem to think so."

"Watch yourself," Ortega said. "I think you don't make friends so easily."

It was good advice. Tibbits, his face flushed with excitement and the dusky light, handed Justice his revolver and hat.

"I think the man's crazy," Tibbits said, nodding at McCulloch's twitching form. "I really think he is."

Ruff holstered the weapon and turned, walking to where the redhead sat on the ground in a muddy, soaking wet dress.

"Better get out of those clothes," Justice said.

"I will. Thanks." Ruff stuck out a hand and pulled her to her feet. "First time anyone ever fought for my honor," she said with a small grin.

"What happened?"

"Nothing much. Jealous wife and a husband with a roving eye." Her tone indicated that it wasn't a new experience for her.

Her red hair was tangled and plastered to her skull. Her green, wide eyes met his, paused there, and then drifted away. She smiled and stood up.

"My name's Taylor Cribbs," the girl said.

"Ruff Justice."

"Oh, I know that," she answered. "I know who you are, Mr. Justice."

She smiled again and walked away. Justice watched her go, hardly able to blame the sodbuster who had initiated all of this.

McCulloch was on his feet now, supported by a man on either side of him. He walked past Justice without seeing him. He was still sailing among the stars.

Justice ran his fingers through his hair, put on his hat, and started back toward the camp himself. The night was coming on fast, and it was too cold to be standing there, wet in the wind.

Leading his pony, he veered to the south of the camp to a second small knoll where a dead, twisted oak stood. He broke some wood from the tree and started a small fire of his own, stripping off his buckskins and hanging them from a tree branch.

He had a spare cotton shirt and a pair of jeans in his saddlebags. He unbuckled them and pulled out the folded shirt. The wind was cool, the night dark. The footsteps behind Justice brought his head around sharply.

"Don't bother about the shirt," Taylor Cribbs said. "You look just fine the way you are."

She came forward, carrying a blanket over her arm, wearing a white blouse and gray skirt. Her red hair, still damp, was brushed out down her back.

"Come on. I'll warm you up, Justice. I owe you that much at least."

"You don't owe me," Justice said. He was naked, standing half in shadow, half in firelight. The girl's eyes swept over him.

"No," she laughed, "I don't owe you a thing—but I'd like to. I'm cold too, you know."

She had begun unbuttoning her white blouse with one hand, smiling as she worked. "You don't want me to catch pneumonia, do you?"

"Keep your blouse on. That'll help."

"Not as much as you can."

Justice took a few steps forward. Her eyes were

bright with firelight, her hair like dark copper. His fingers rose to finish unbuttoning the blouse. She wore nothing underneath.

Full, healthy breasts bobbed from her blouse. The pink nipples were erect and inviting. Taylor saw Ruff's eyes roaming her body, and she laughed out loud.

"Come on, Justice, warm me properly."

They spread the blanket on the ground near the small fire. The oak was stark against the starry sky. Ruff Justice lay down and waited as the woman slipped from her skirt—there was nothing else under that either. He watched her walk to him, and go to her knees. She bent low to kiss his chest, his lips, his flat abdomen, his inner thighs. Her hands found his growing erection and cradled it.

Taylor lifted herself and threw a leg over Justice, straddling him, her eyes still bright with firelight—or want or need. . . . She slowly lifted herself and positioned his shaft, sinking onto him, her warmth surrounding him as she bent forward, her hair veiling her face and breasts. She kissed Justice deeply, shuddered, and settled against him, her breath soft and rapid against his face.

Ruff reached around her, clenching her smooth, firm buttocks, his thumbs resting in the cleft. He held her to him as she began to pitch and quiver, her body heated and trembling.

Taylor arched her neck, cupped her own breast, and offered it to Justice. His lips went to her nipple, teasing it, and Taylor moaned softly, deeply.

Justice took her head and pulled it down to his mouth, crushing his lips against hers, holding the kiss while she thrashed on top of him. Justice began to thrust deeper, lifting his body to her rhythm—steady, quick, demanding—until Taylor gave a startled gasp and collapsed against him, her lips finding his ear, neck, and mouth.

A second time she began to move, working her body against his mechanically, her pelvis nearly bruising his as Justice felt his own need rising. Taylor reached in back of her and found Ruff's shaft where it entered her. She moaned again and began stroking him, her body lunging at his, needing his completion.

Justice came with a sudden rush, and Taylor sighed, leaning forward again to kiss him, to whisper into his ear.

Justice lay relaxed and heated, his thumping heart slowing at last. He let her kiss him, touch him, run her hands across his chest and shoulders.

Suddenly he moved, rolling to one side. Taylor started to cry out, but Ruff clamped his hand over her mouth.

There was someone out there. Someone on horseback. The muffled hoofbeats drifted on the wind. Justice glanced at the low burning fire, gestured for Taylor to stay where she was, and then snatched up his Colt.

Naked, he moved into the night, circling away from the oak.

He crouched, feeling the night wind against his body, scenting the things that belonged to the night, the dew of the grass and the dark earth. An owl flashed low across the star-filled sky, and Ruff's eyes followed it briefly.

He moved on down the knoll to the edge of the creek, his feet silent.

The horseman loomed up out of the night, a dark figure on a dark horse. The horse suddenly reared, seeing Justice, and Ruff leaped, trying to grab its reins.

The rider kicked out viciously at Ruff, his boot glancing off Justice's hand. Justice clawed out with his left hand as the rearing horse lunged forward, leaping into a run, but all he caught was air as the horse's haunch brushed against him and the rider made his escape across the creek.

Panting, Justice watched him go. The night swallowed up horse and rider, and Ruff turned back toward the oak tree where Taylor stood waiting, hastily dressed, her hair a profuse red tangle.

"Who was it?" she asked in a small, breathless voice.

"I don't know," he answered. Not for sure, he didn't.

"Why would anyone come around the camp like that?"

"To look us over," Ruff said, reaching for his pants. "To see what kind of security we have, maybe."

"Someone like Dan Court, you mean."

Justice nodded. "Someone exactly like Dan Court."

Justice wasn't telling her that to scare her, nor was he guessing entirely. He hadn't seen the man's face at all. But the horse was a different matter—it was hard to miss the mayor of Bismarck's big bay.

"Why is he still following us . . . if it is him?" Taylor watched as Justice pulled on his shirt and buttoned it. "How long can a man stay mad?"

"A lifetime," Justice answered. But he didn't think Court was mad any longer. Court wanted everything these settlers might have, nothing more. And from what the marshal had told them about big Dan Court, Justice had the idea he wouldn't balk at killing them to get it. Every last one of them.

Justice was seated, pulling on his boots. He would

rather have been rolled up in his blankets, sleeping with Taylor Cribbs, but he knew neither of them would be able to sleep again that night.

The redhead stood by, her arms folded beneath her breasts, shivering a little.

"Why are you going to Deadwater?" Ruff asked.

She smiled slowly, her eyes brightening. "Trying to find out all my secrets already?"

"I'm just interested. It's the edge of nowhere, the end of the line. For someone without a promise of something, it's a long gamble, isn't it?"

"We take gambles." Taylor shrugged.

"Mostly people do that when they have to." Ruff stood, buckling his gunbelt.

"Maybe I have to," Taylor said quietly.

"What happened?"

She shrugged again, a small, almost defensive gesture. "A man was killed," she answered. "I did it."

"For the hell of it?"

Her smile deepened briefly. "Sure. I'm a wild-eyed, gunslinging killer. No, Justice, not for the hell of it. He was a gambler and the owner of a saloon. I worked for him, and he thought that meant he owned me. . . . He didn't."

"Is there paper out on you? A murder warrant?"

"I don't know. Maybe. He came after me. I shot him. It was terrible. Seeing someone die in front of you, someone you've killed . . . I ran out of the room and kept running."

"What about your friends?"

"Dolly and Priscilla? They're just people I met here. Other women at the end of their rope, I guess. They knew me for what I was, so I took up with them. No one else wanted anything to do with me, that's for sure. What I am, Justice—it shows."

"It shows," Ruff said, stepping toward her to hold her briefly, "and it's damned attractive. Don't let people like McCulloch get you down. You're better than he is."

"I'd like to think so."

"Believe it," Justice said. "Tell yourself that it's true and keep on telling yourself."

"I'd rather have you keep telling me, Ruff Justice. You say it better."

She kissed him once, lightly, and turned, walking away toward the night camp below them. Justice watched her go. Then slowly he turned to face the man behind him.

"Nice-looking lady," Tom Beers said.

"She's carrying a load," Justice told the Texas cowboy.

"Yeah. Seems like everyone on this wagon train is carrying a load." Beers rolled and lit a cigarette. "Pathetic bunch, ain't we?"

"Just a lot of people looking for a second chance."

"What about that rider who was snooping around?" Beers asked. The tiny red ember of his cigarette danced in front of his lips.

"You saw him?"

"Heard him first, then saw you having a ruckus. Then it was over. I didn't think you wanted him shot. Probably couldn't have hit him in the night on that moving horse anyway."

"I'm pretty sure it was Dan Court."

"Still wants his war, does he?"

"He does. Beers, we're going to have to watch out. Court will be back. As soon as he figures we're far enough from town and the fort, he'll be back."

"Yes, sir, Mr. Justice," the cowboy answered. "You're right. He will be back. And then someone's going to get hurt." He amended that. "Someone is going to get dead."

Justice didn't answer. Beers was absolutely right. Someone was going to get dead, maybe a lot of people, and there just wasn't much Ruff Justice could do about it. Nothing for now but watch and wait and keep his guns loaded.

8

Morning dawned gray and windy. Clouds were building in the north, and the sun pierced the silver sky with sabers of gold. Justice stared gloomily at the clouds and at the wagon train camp below, where the grumbling, cursing, wooden-limbed settlers had begun hitching their teams. They were all weary this morning—most of them were city people, unused to this sort of travel. Their bottoms were sore from wooden wagon seats, their hands cramped and blistered from gripping the reins as they guided their teams through the long, jolting, dusty day.

Ruff Justice wasn't in such good repair himself; a few more hours sleep wouldn't have bothered him a bit.

McCulloch, on horseback, found Justice on the knoll. The big man had a nasty bruise on his face; his eyes were red and angry. He reined up beside Justice, scowling. Justice recognized the horse—it was Will Handy's.

"Come up to say let's let bygones be bygones," McCulloch said. "I lose my temper sometimes. I wouldn't have hurt the girl."

"All right," Justice answered stiffly.

"I hear Dan Court was around last night," McCulloch said. The horse shifted its feet and blew through its nostrils.

"It seems like he was."

"Damn. I wish we'd of . . ." McCulloch avoided saying it again. He wished they had ridden over that night and eliminated Court and his people. It was the mirror image of Court's own philosophy. "I'll be riding flank today myself."

"Will Handy driving your wagon?" Justice asked.

"That's right. Something wrong with that?"

"No. Just asking. You've never met this Will Handy before, have you?"

"Never. But he's a good man."

So good that he'd wanted to shoot Justice the day before. For what reason? Fighting with a man he had known for less than twenty-four hours. Either Will Handy made attachments easily, or there was something more to know about him.

"Want me to ride with you?" McCulloch asked.

"No, thanks."

"Kind of a loner, aren't you . . . except when it comes to women," he couldn't resist adding.

"I'm kind of a loner" was all Justice said.

He watched McCulloch ride off and then walked down to the camp. Almost everyone was ready to go, but Ortega and the cowboys still stood around their fire, drinking coffee. Justice wanted a cup.

"Good morning," Ortega said. He was smiling as he sipped his coffee, his eyes bright with pleasure. "Sleep well, Ruff Justice?"

It seemed everyone in the camp knew about Taylor Cribbs and Ruff. Justice just grunted, crouched, and poured himself a cup of strong, bitter coffee.

"Any particular plan?" Tom Beers asked.

"Keep your eyes open, that's all."

"That I intend to do. How far to Deadwater now, Justice?" the cowboy asked.

"A day and a half." Justice looked up at the clouded skies. "If it doesn't rain."

"Then he'll have to hit us soon, won't he?"

"Maybe. Maybe he intends to let us get there—why would he want to cart these goods in?"

"I hadn't thought of that," Beers said.

Ortega was still smiling, but some of the humor had left his smile. "Sure," he said, "we carry it there for him. Then he takes it. A new town, Deadwater. New people, new businesses. Maybe he starts the new graveyard, eh?"

Maybe so—that might just be the way Court was going to do it. Justice finished his coffee, and returned the cup. He walked to where his spotted horse, cranky and cold, was waiting.

And Mary Caffiter watched him go. The little old lady in blue gingham wearing a huge sunbonnet. The little old lady who hated Ruff Justice for having taken her son's life.

Justice barely glanced at Mary Caffiter.

What was there in Deadwater for her? Justice wondered. A place to finish out a bitter life, some wish or dream? Or was she just like the rest of the lost people in this wagon train—traveling to the end of the line because there was no other chance, and no point in remaining behind in an empty world.

Justice saddled up and rode out away from the wagon train and its people. The wind was turning hard and cold. The long grass was nearly blue, shuddering and bending as Justice led his spotted pony westward, to where the land rose and became wooded.

He saw no other sentries. There was no sign of McCulloch, and that suited Justice just fine.

He lifted his eyes to the highlands, toward Deadwater, knowing he still couldn't see it at this distance. Susan Donner was there; Susan still had to be told that her man was dead.

"Damn it, Colonel MacEnroe," Justice muttered, "you do give me the good ones."

At noon he watered his horse at a narrow rill which trickled off the piny slopes beyond and above him. It was there that Justice found the tracks.

He had been looking for sign all day—for sign left by Dan Court or by the lone rider who had sniped at him. He had found nothing at all. But here, in the mud beside the rill, he found the tracks of a horse and of a man.

A man in moccasins.

It had to be an Indian, and there was nothing too threatening about that. The Swamp Cheyenne were the only local group, and they were generally peaceful. Still, it was possible that Stone Eyes and his hostile followers had drifted back into the area. Justice slowly looked around, seeing no one, nothing but a cawing crow drifting on the wind.

It was another long minute before it hit him. Ruff had half turned away from the tracks in the mud; now he turned back, his eyebrows drawing together in puzzlement.

That wasn't right at all.

The moccasin tracks seemed too familiar, and then Justice's brain sorted out the reason. They were Apache moccasins.

"You must be dreaming, Justice," he said to himself. His horse pricked its ears and looked at him as if he were mad. Maybe he was.

"You're in trouble when you start seeing Apache sign in Dakota." Still—Ruff hunkered down again. He was no stranger to the Apache. He had spent time down on the border fighting them. He could have sworn . . . but there was no figuring it.

"Must be losing it," Justice said. "My imagination's working overtime."

But usually imagination provides something plausible to work with. This wasn't plausible. Unless some trapper or local Indian had somehow, for some reason, traded for a pair of Apache high moccasins. . . . That had to be it.

The horse had had enough to drink, so Justice started on again, swinging aboard into a blast of northern wind. It was going to rain; there was no doubt about it. He could smell the rain on the wind, feel the electricity in the air.

It wouldn't help the wagon train at all. Court would be able to move around more easily, and the wagons would slow and possibly have to stop. Justice had started away from the creek, but now he reined up, hesitated, and turned back. It wouldn't hurt to follow those tracks for a while.

The horse the man in moccasins was riding left clear tracks. Justice followed them, unsheathing his rifle just in case, tucking the sheath under his thigh while holding the cool, deadly, big-bore Spencer repeater in his hand. He was inexplicably on edge now, feeling something he couldn't come to grips with—or maybe it was just his body's reaction to the oncoming storm, to the pressure changes and electrical disturbances.

Maybe.

The man in moccasins had ridden due west. Not

toward the Swamp Cheyenne camp on the Flame River to the south, but due west.

Toward Deadwater.

Justice was now in the trees, among the scattered pines and live oak. The ground was littered with pine needles and dry oak leaves, cartwheeling through the air with each fresh gust of wind.

The tracks were gone.

Perhaps he could have tried to pick them up again, but there was no real justification for following this man, whoever he was, to wherever he was going—which seemed to be the ghost town of Deadwater.

Besides, Justice had spotted something that intrigued him more.

The smoke rose, wavering and wispy, whipped away by the wind at times, but it was coming from the south. The smoke wasn't anywhere near the Indian camp.

It had to be Dan Court.

Justice started in that direction, circling wide to the west, climbing higher through the pines which grew denser and taller now. Once, through a gap in the trees, he got a glimpse of the distant Flame River, roaring and frothing its way downslope.

It was a bad river, an angry river. Once, not so long ago, Ruff had had a time of it on the Flame. He turned his eyes away.

The smoke was on his left now, to the east, and he started downslope, figuring that Court wouldn't be looking for company from this direction.

He was going to get some.

Justice had a little surprise party in mind—assuming Court and fate cooperated. The wind creaked through the pines, and rain began to fall in large, occasional drops.

The camp was just below Ruff. He halted his horse and sat watching the activity. Seven or eight men were visible, most of them gathered around a fire. Something was cooking in a black iron pot over a low flame. Court ran an easy camp: there was time for a noon meal and chatter.

Exactly what Justice could do was nebulous at best, but he could put the fear of God into them. Maybe with a little luck he could cut their numbers down a little.

He slipped from the saddle, looped the spotted horse's reins around a low-hanging oak limb, and got to his belly, levering a round into the Spencer's breech.

The first shot took a man in a red shirt through the arm, nearly severing it. He screamed and spun around, falling into the cookfire. The iron pot spilled its boiling contents on him, and there was a sudden mad rush for cover.

A second man failed to make it to the trees. Justice's big .56 spoke again, and the man collapsed, his spine sawn through by a death-dealing 500 grain bullet.

Ruff saw the big man in the faded blue shirt just a little too late, and as he sighted on Court himself, the raider leaped behind a fallen log. Ruff's bullet plowed through the bark of the log, spraying fragments into the air.

Now the guns from below began to echo the thunder of the big .56. Half a dozen rifles answered his shots, seeking flesh and blood. Justice pulled away from the rim of the hill, moved in a crouch to the uneasy spotted pony, and mounted as the Winchesters below peppered the woods with lead.

That was enough. Maybe just enough to let Court know it wasn't going to be so easy, maybe enough to run off some of his recruits who might not be so eager to give up their lives for a wagonload of stolen goods.

Justice continued to circle, riding south through a long, rocky valley and up over a pine-studded crest before striking out toward the wagon train. By the time he reached the wagons, it was pouring rain. Gusting, bitter winds drove the steady silver ribbons of rainwater out of the cold, gray skies.

McCulloch was in a foul mood.

"Where in hell have you been?" he shouted above the wind.

"Trying to do my job."

"You'd a-done it right, it wouldn't have happened," McCulloch yelled. He said something else Ruff didn't get above the wind.

"What happened?"

"Why, damn it, Justice—the Indians. Indians hit us back a mile. We lost three people, one of 'em a woman."

"How many Indians? Where'd they come from?"

"I don't know where they came from. There was only about a dozen. The greaser shot two; one of them cowboys tagged another. They came right out of the rain, rode through our ranks shooting left and right. Tagged an ox first off, and when it went down, a wagon spilled. Goddammit, Justice, you're supposed to be a scout. You're supposed to know what's going on. You're supposed—"

"Shut up."

"What did you say?" McCulloch puffed up. Ruff saw his hands tighten on the rifle he was carrying.

"I said shut up. The rain's getting worse. We're going to have to pull up and circle. It doesn't do any good in the world for you to yell at me. Let's get organized, set up a defense, and then someone can tell me what happened. Then I'll tell you why I couldn't be in two places at once."

The wagons were bogging down badly as the rain began to saturate the prairie soil. It wasn't easy trying to get things organized, trying to form a halfway decent circle.

Justice was particular about things. He made a few more enemies making sure those wagons were pushed close together. If the wagon train had been hit by Indians, they could only be Stone Eyes's Cheyenne renegades. And if it was Stone Eyes, he was sure to be back. He was a man with a holy vision—the death of all whites. Elusive, murderous, and clever, Stone Eyes had raised hell on the Dakota plains for years. He was the man Colonel MacEnroe wanted above all others.

Stone Eyes had been raised on a reservation. Apparently he hadn't been treated well and hadn't taken to the white man's harness. He had killed a missionary and made a break for free country, taking a handful of followers with him. He'd only been a kid at the time. Later, as his raids became more extensive, and successful, other dissatisfied Cheyenne and some Sioux had flocked to his standard.

MacEnroe had pursued him to the border and then lost him frustratingly. It now appeared that the Canadians had had enough of Stone Eyes and had chased him back to Dakota; or perhaps the Cheyenne renegade had had another bloody vision.

One thing was certain; if McCulloch had seen a dozen warriors, there had to be another dozen behind them. And probably another dozen. And another.

And right in their path lay Deadwater.

Justice was riding with his usual luck. It was raining and cold. He had white raiders to the south and Stone Eyes to the north. Aside from a single sleek redheaded lady, he was generally unliked by the settlers. An Apache was riding the plains inexplicably, and a sniper who wore ladies' gloves had already taken a shot at him.

Things could have been better.

Lightning arced across the sky, and the rain began to fall in cold buckets. Ruff Justice lifted his eyes and winked at the malicious spirits of the sky. They must be having a hell of a laugh up there somewhere.

9

The faces around the campfire were grim, bright in the shifting flames, screened by the cold falling rain which had now settled in for good.

"Why did we stop—we'd've been better off to keep rolling, if you ask me," the narrow-eyed settler named Daniels said.

"Think so?" Ruff Justice asked. "You try fighting from a moving wagon in the rain."

"We'd be bogged down by now anyway," Ortega put in.

"What are we supposed to do then? Just sit here and wait for this renegade to hit us again?"

"That's right," Justice replied. "That's about all there is to do."

"Damn all, if—"

Justice was tired of the man. He hadn't contributed anything but gripes. "What did you think you'd find out here?" he asked. "Milk and honey? You must have known how things were in Dakota. You must have made a decision to come anyway, to fight for what you wanted. Now you're going to have to fight. It's that simple."

"Sure they'll be back, Justice?" Tom Beers asked.

The Texan was smoking; how he kept that thing burning in the rain was anybody's guess.

"Yes, they'll be back. We've got too much stuff they can use. Guns, ammunition, horses and oxen, food supplies, blankets . . . women."

"How many?"

"That's the big question. Are they trickling down from up north, slowly massing, or traveling in one large band? I'd guess they're traveling in small bands for safety, planning on massing somewhere—what for, I don't know. Maybe Stone Eyes figures he finally has enough people to challenge the army head-on."

"You didn't answer the question exactly, Justice."

"A guess? Two dozen to a hundred."

"That's not very precise, is it?" McCulloch asked belligerently. He and Will Handy stood together, rain dripping from their hat brims.

"Not very," Justice responded. "There's only one way to know for sure—ride out to their camp and ask."

"If we could spot their camp—"

"In this weather? Cheyenne?" Ruff smiled. "Try it and get back to us, will you?"

"Then what the hell are we supposed to do?" McCulloch asked in frustration.

"What we're doing. Form up, be ready, hope the rain stops."

McCulloch walked away grumbling. Ortega told Justice, "This is not a good place to die, my friend."

"They don't make any good places, Felipe."

Tom Beers lit yet another smoke. "I wish you men would quit talkin' that way. I'm not ready to go out, and I don't intend to."

One of the other cowboys suggested, "We could ride out, Tom. Wagons might be bogged down, but a man on horseback could make it through to Deadwater."

"Forget that. We signed on with this bunch." Beers's eyes flashed briefly, then his easy grin returned. "What do you want us to do, Justice?"

"Drag what you can out of these wagons. Heavy stuff. Fill in between the wagons."

"Barricades. You really do think they'll be coming."

"Let's not take any chances. We can shove everything back in when the rain stops."

"Folks won't like it."

Justice said, "We'll have to remind 'em they won't like being dead much either."

Ruff started walking the perimeter of the camp, talking to the men. He sent every other man to bed. There was no sense in all of them standing watch, and everyone being dog-tired. For a time he stood watching the storm, the slanting rain pale red and gold before the still-burning campfire. Ortega was right. This was no place to die, but it looked as if someone might die here very soon.

Twelve Cheyenne. Maybe that was all there were; maybe they were raiders broken off from Stone Eyes's main band.

They could always hope it was true.

"You'll catch cold."

Ruff turned slowly. He had been standing behind Taylor Cribbs's wagon without realizing it. She peered out from the canvas, her hair down, wearing a nightdress and wrapper.

"Hello, Taylor."

"Trying to sneak around and see me?"

"No, but it's a good idea," Justice replied.

"Climb up for a minute—quietly. The kids are sleeping."

Ruff nodded and clambered aboard. A family called Schoendienst had given Taylor a ride. Their two blond kids lay under a stack of comforters and blankets in the corner, a boy and a girl, ages three and five.

"Cute, huh?"

"Very cute," Ruff Justice replied, but his eyes had shifted to Taylor's. She was very cute as well—cute and appealing, her breasts forming enticing mounds beneath the faded blue wrapper.

"Not tonight, I guess," Taylor said with a sigh.

"No, not tonight."

Ruff perched on a trunk, looking around the wagon. A few pieces of furniture, Schoendienst's spare harnesses, food stuffs, his carpenter's tools.

"They treat you right, do they?"

"They're good people, Ruffin. I guess they're the kind a town needs when it's building. Them"—she nodded toward the kids—"they can't talk of anything else but the house their daddy is going to build for them in Deadwater. They're from the East—lived in some kind of little flat or whatever you call it. The old man's a carpenter, but he was working in a shoe factory—alongside kids ten, twelve years old. He got to looking at them, thinking about his own kids, thinking where he was going. He came home and told his wife they were leaving—for anywhere.

"Mrs. Schoendienst was so pleased she burst into tears. Anything, she told him, was better than living where they were."

"I hope so," Ruff Justice said quietly.

"The Indians?"

"Yes. The Indians, and Dan Court. Don't forget about Dan Court."

"I haven't forgotten him for a minute. I saw him up

close when he was mad. Crazy eyes. Justice"—she stepped closer, her waist at his eye level. She put her long smooth arms around his neck—"you'll get us out of this, won't you?"

"I'm going to try like hell." Ruff held her for a moment. His body started getting ideas as her nearness, the scent and touch of her, began to work on him. "Better get going," he said.

Taylor sighed and stepped back, hands on hips, head cocked to one side. The rain was tapping furiously on the canvas top. One of the kids turned, muttered something, and rolled over again before settling to sleep.

The flap of canvas in the back of the wagon opened, and Schoendienst himself peered in. He was tall, long-jawed, and just now very shaken.

"Justice, thank God. They're looking everywhere for you—the Cheyenne are coming in."

Justice snatched up his rifle and slid from the wagon. He glanced at the fire, but it had gone out. Either the rain had done it, or one of the wiser settlers had put it out. It was dark as sin and raining to beat the band.

Schoendienst led Ruff to where Ortega, Beers, and McCulloch were waiting, hunched behind a barricade of barrels and crates. Their heads came around.

"Where?" Ruff asked.

Ortega pointed. "Can't see them now. When lightning struck awhile ago, I saw two of them in the coulee north of us."

The coulee was no more than a hundred feet away. By now the Cheyenne would be even closer. And there were damn sure more than two of them.

"Want me to roust everyone?" Beers asked.

"Yes. Quietly."

"My God," McCulloch snarled, "how are we going to fight them if we can't see them?"

"You'll see them," Justice answered grimly.

He looked around at the defenses of the wagon train. Adequate, he supposed. At least the Indians wouldn't be able to burn the wagons on a night like this. Across the circle he could see men moving into position. Tibbits in dark coat and pants carrying a shotgun. Will Handy. And standing beside them was the old woman, Mary Caffiter, ready to load.

"Look out!"

It was Ortega who shouted but Tom Beers who pulled his trigger first. The painted Cheyenne had reared up not ten feet away from them, bringing his feather-decorated rifle to his shoulder.

Beers used his handgun. A spinning .44 slug slapped at the Indian's chest, ripping a gaping hole where it exited, and the Indian went down, a war cry dying in his throat.

The Indians were suddenly everywhere, storm demons rushing at them out of the hiss and roar of the rain. Thunder spoke as the settlers' guns opened up. One of Beers's cowboys went down in the first rush, a bullet gnawing its way into his eye and out the back of his skull. The cowboy cartwheeled backward and lay still. A woman's scream hung in the air.

Ruff Justice hunkered down behind a crate and opened up with his thunder gun. The .56 spat flame and death into the night. He might have gotten a hit, but he wasn't sure.

It was a weird and murky battle. Indians loomed up out of the darkness and then were swallowed up by the storm. Targets appeared and vanished as shots were fired. Lightning struck occasionally, and then the dozens of Cheyenne renegades were briefly, clearly visible; ghostly white, eerily painted with zig-zag stripes and bloody handprints.

Then the lightning flickered out, and there was nothing at all but the lash of the wind and rain.

Ruff settled in and kept firing. Anything at all was a target out there, anything a hostile Indian. He fired once at a dark shadow—no more than a cloud stain on the earth—and heard the scream of pain from a living thing.

"Fire at their muzzle flashes," he reminded the others. McCulloch emptied his seventeen-shot needle gun inside of a minute, firing at ghosts. The big man was haggard, badly frightened.

He had the right.

The first Cheyenne leaped into the camp on the back of a pinto pony. He had a handgun, and he fired left and right as he rode straight through the settlers. Tibbits was hit, but his shotgun had triggered off, bringing the Indian and his pony down in a wash of flame.

Tibbits didn't move. The horse didn't move. The Indian lay crushed and still beneath it.

"Here they come!" someone yelled from the other side.

Ruff shouted to Ortega, "You and Beers stay here." Justice was off at a run to the opposite side of the camp.

They were coming all right. Out of the rain and night came seven, eight, ten mounted Indians, their guns slashing at the wagon train in a rapid-fire barrage.

Splinters were ripped from the wagon to the left of Ruff's head. Another bullet whined off a wagon tongue strap. Ruff sighted and fired. The .56, designed to stop a bull buffalo, stopped a war pony in its tracks, and the brave riding it went down in a heap. Justice shot him as he rose to continue the attack on foot.

The settler beside Justice said, "Good shot. We'll teach—"

He was beyond teaching. A bullet from somewhere ripped his throat open, and he was flung back to lie against the earth, strangling on his own blood.

Ruff sighted in on another target, shifting his position slightly. He never got that shot off. As he shifted for a better line of fire, a bullet thudded into the wagon planks beside him.

From behind.

Justice spun, and his eyes immediately found a second target. Will Handy wasn't twenty feet away from him. His rifle was curling smoke; his lip was curled back. Handy jacked a second cartridge into the breech of his Winchester, but he was too slow about it.

Ruff's .56 belched flame and death. The bullet nearly cut Handy in two. Ruff saw him fall and then turned his attention back to the Indian charge.

He plucked one Cheyenne from his horse's back and missed a shot at a second as the warrior went down behind his pony's shoulder. Then they were gone. All of them. The night had whisked them away into the storm. There was only the lingering scent of burnt gunpowder, the drumming of the rain, and the moans of the injured.

Ruff rose slowly, reloading his rifle. Then he turned and walked to where Will Handy lay on his back, holding his belly.

McCulloch was coming on the run. "They got Handy?"

"Yeah," Justice said, saving the explanation.

"Is he dead?" the wagon master asked.

Ruff crouched down beside the man they knew as Will Handy. "Not yet," Ruff replied. The rain fell steadily, more lightly now, and Ruff could barely make out the man's face—his white eyes, and moving, cracked lips.

"Figured it . . ." Handy said.

"Who are you?"

"Figured it finally . . . nearly got you."

"What's your name?" Justice asked again.

"Pabst. Wiley Pabst."

Ruff knew the name, but he had never met the man before. "Why'd you want me, Wiley?"

"Finally figured it out. . . ."

"Somebody pay you to do it?"

"Sure . . . why else? Me and Jud Hollister . . . Apache."

"*What* Apache?" Ruff demanded.

Pabst moaned. The pain in his guts was like a fire storm. "Figured it . . . what a laugh . . ." Then Pabst did laugh, or tried to. A horrible gurgling sound emerged from his lips, along with a bloody froth.

"Who paid you, Pabst?" Ruff demanded.

"Woman . . . Conklin. Pete Conklin."

"Conklin's dead," Ruff said.

"Woman paid us. Me . . . Hollister . . . Apache."

And then his lips stopped moving. His eyes stared up at the cold rain; unseeing, unfeeling.

"Who was he?" McCulloch demanded. "What was he talking about?"

"Better see to the wounded," Justice said, standing. "Tell everyone the Cheyenne will likely be back." Then he turned his back deliberately on McCulloch and walked away into the rain. Ruff was disturbed, preoccupied, and badly puzzled.

"Pabst," he muttered to the night storm, "you could

have at least done me the favor of living another few minutes." Things had only gotten more complicated. Pabst hadn't so much explained things as muddled them up. Unless . . .

There wasn't time to follow his line of thought. Ortega yelled, "Here they come again," and Ruff started for the barricades as the bullets began to fly once more.

10

The night was a bloody, smoke-and-rain-filled vigil. The Cheyenne appeared, broke off their attack, and settled into sniping, which cost the settlers three more lives and as many wounded, one of them a child.

They waited in the cold and the rain and prayed for dawn. When dawn did come, it was only a slow graying of the black mass of clouds in the east. The rain still fell, the wind still blew.

A morning fire was kindled with difficulty, and coffee boiled in two-quart pots. Ruff was sipping coffee from a tin cup at his post, leaning wearily against the wagon, when the old woman with a gun in her hand walked up to him.

"Good morning, Mrs. Caffiter."

Mary Caffiter didn't respond. She looked very old, washed out. Her dress hung limply on her time-eroded frame. She had shed her bonnet, and her gray hair, pinned tightly to her skull, was thin and damp.

"I hope you're not going to use that gun," Ruff Justice said mildly. He sipped at his coffee again, staring down at the tiny, soulless woman.

"It's one of Ortega's. I've been reloading for him,"

Mary Caffiter said. She looked at the pistol oddly, as if surprised that she still held it.

"It's been a long night—you ought to get yourself some rest," Justice suggested.

"A long night." She looked to the paling skies, seeing a brief flash of golden light before the storm took it away again. "A long life. A long and sorrowful life, Mr. Justice," she said.

"It's not always easy."

"It's never easy. Never!" Her voice rose, cracked, and then dropped again. "We might die here."

"Or we might die a mile down the road. Today, tomorrow, the next day. But think of all the times we've scraped by, the times we didn't die. Hell, we're lucky to have made it this far, all of us."

She didn't seem to hear anything he had said. She repeated, "We might die here. I don't want to carry this bitterness to my grave. I don't want it on my soul, Mr. Justice."

"Anger just carves up the one who carries it, Mrs. Caffiter. It's a useless emotion."

"It's hard for a mother . . . hard to *see* her children."

"Sure it is."

"I know what Billy Lane Caffiter was. I know he was no good. A killer."

Ruff was silent. The woman was groping for words as if working her way through a field of high grass, searching for daylight.

"He was a killer, and I knew it inside, but I wouldn't admit it. He was . . . my baby. How can you admit to yourself that your baby is a murderer who deserves to be hung?"

Ruff shook his head. A sound behind him turned his eyes briefly, but it was only the wind in the grass.

Mary Caffiter went on, "I don't want to die with

hatred in my heart, Mr. Justice. You shot Billy Lane and killed him. People told me what happened—that it was self-defense, that he had been on a rampage, hurting other people that night—but I didn't choose to believe it. I didn't want to know what he was.

"Deep down I knew, though. I knew. I pretended it wasn't so, and that meant I had to find someone, something to blame for his death. I blamed you.

"Now," she said, shaking her head nervously, her eyes gazing past Justice into the distant reaches, "I don't blame you. I suppose . . . I suppose you did the world a favor when you shot Billy Lane Caffiter."

And then she went away—a tiny, hunched, wispy woman with a clear conscience and an empty heart. Justice returned to his watching.

To his watching and his thinking.

Jud Hollister, Wiley Pabst . . . and the Apache?

Who in hell was the Apache? It fit with the odd tracks Justice had found the day before. Apache moccasin prints in the river mud. Was he another hunter, another hired killer?

Ruff took the jack of diamonds with the bullet hole through it from his pocket. That had bothered him—a single playing card. Why does a man carry a single card around with him? The answer Justice came up with was a cold-blooded one, and he didn't much care for it.

"Gambling," he told himself. "Cutting cards for the privilege . . . of killing Ruffin T. Justice."

Hollister had won. And then lost. Wiley Pabst had made his try. Presumably if Pabst failed, the Apache was left to have his chance.

Just who hated him that much? Enough to hire not one but three killers and pay them all—Hollister had been carrying three hundred in gold. Pabst had nothing like that, but they had found some newly minted gold eagles on him when they carried the body from the camp.

Who?

Pabst had said it was a woman. *He* had figured it out, he said. Justice couldn't. The only name mentioned had been that of Pete Conklin, but Conklin was dead along with his brothers Jacob and Wesley. Justice had been there when they died.

Justice had made certain that they died.

That dispute had started on the Pine Ridge reservation. Colonel MacEnroe had sent Justice over to help out the Indian agent, a man named Sam Shore. It seemed that the three Conklin brothers had been selling poison whisky to the Indians. Six men had died as a result of it. The Conklins themselves drank whisky—if better stuff—and a lot of it.

They had decided to have some fun with a young Indian woman. They had so much fun with her that she died.

Justice had tracked the three to an old French fort. Nothing was left standing but the blockhouse and the still the brothers had made. Ruff had asked them to surrender, but they would have none of it. After a three-hour siege, Justice had fired the building, still calling for them to come out.

They didn't and they had died in the flames, screaming and cursing, firing their guns at the smoke. Justice had left what remained of the brothers there and had ridden off. It hadn't been much fun knowing the Conklin brothers.

Was there another brother? A sister or mother . . . the woman's gloves still troubled him. . . .

"Here they come. South side!" Tom Beers shouted,

and Justice set his tin cup down and snuggled up to the stock of the .56 once again.

In the morning attack McCulloch took an arrow in his right shoulder. During the night the Indians had spirited away six horses, and McCulloch, discovering this, had left the wagon circle to bring some of the other stock in closer. He had paid for it.

Schoendienst was killed by an Indian bullet. His wife's crying could be heard throughout the camp.

The rain broke at midmorning, and the sun emerged, bright and yawning. As if by magic, the Cheyenne disappeared. They were gone, utterly gone; even their dead had been carried away. Only two dead ponies remained to mark their passage.

"Bastards, bastards, bastards . . ." McCulloch kept moaning. His shirt had been ripped open, and a bandage had been knotted around his wound. His arm was swollen and was turning colors.

"Will they be back again?" Ortega asked. His dark face was stained even darker with powder smoke and grime.

"*Quién sabe*, Felipe?" Justice shrugged. "We might have given them enough . . . or they could have decided to wait for reinforcements. I think we ought to get moving."

"With the few animals we have left?" McCulloch complained. "We'd have to leave three wagons."

"Want to stay here and wait for Stone Eyes?" Ruff asked.

"No," the wagon master muttered, "I guess not. Christ, Justice, we're already traveling double. Know what kind of a load those wagons will be carrying— and over muddy ground?"

"Justice knows," Tom Beers said.

"And doesn't give a damn—neither do you. Hell,

you're on horseback. How are we supposed to carry our goods?"

"You'll just have to leave some behind," Justice said. "Able-bodied people will have to walk."

"We can't leave our tools, our goods . . ."

"You'll leave something. Or die for them," Ruff Justice told him. "You decide how you want to do it, but do it. Some of your people are carrying furniture and books, iron stoves. I hate to tell them this, but that sort of thing is going to have to be dumped and left for the Indians. They can make new furniture; they'll have a hell of a time carving out a new skin for themselves. Tell them straight how it has to be. With only the essentials on board, these wagons should still be able to roll."

"And you want me to tell them this?" McCulloch asked.

"You're the man who wanted to be wagon master."

Then Justice walked away before McCulloch had time to form up his ugly thoughts and put words to them.

Ruff found Taylor Cribbs at the Schoendienst wagon. Inside Justice could hear Mrs. Schoendienst, sobbing brokenheartedly.

"Sorry" was all Ruff could say.

Taylor shook her head. "It's a damn shame. She's torn up pretty badly."

"How're the kids taking it?"

"They're crying because she's crying." Taylor shrugged. "I don't think they really understand."

"Take care of them, Taylor. We're moving out. Think you can drive this wagon?"

"If I have to."

"Fine. I'll help you get hitched."

"Justice?"

He turned to look into her troubled deep green eyes, eyes which searched his questioningly. "Are we all crazy? Are we riding straight to hell? Are we all going to die out here?"

"Not if I can help it. We'll get through. Tomorrow you'll be settled into a little white bungalow in Deadwater."

"A saloon crib, more likely," she said, briefly bitter.

"I said a bungalow," Justice repeated. He lifted her chin with his finger, kissed her dry lips lightly, and went looking for Schoendienst's oxen.

He got Taylor hitched, checked a bad pin on the yoke, and blew her a kiss, missing whatever she called to him as he walked away. The wind was still blowing hard as the clouds scudded rapidly across the sky, forming darting shadows on the prairie.

He swung aboard the spotted pony and found Ortega and Beers helping a settler family unload their goods from an overcrowded wagon.

"I'm going to do a little scouting," Justice told them.

"Want company?" Beers asked.

"Not this time. I'm riding west, toward that broken peak. If I don't come back, find another route."

"Think they're really gone?" Beers wanted to know.

"That's what I intend to find out. Don't get too far from your guns."

"Not likely," Beers said dryly. Then he stood and watched as Justice turned his horse and started out past the line of wagons forming onto the plains. "Crazy bastard, but I like him," Beers said to the Mexican.

"Crazy bastard," Felipe Ortega agreed. Then, hunching his shoulders, he got back to work.

Justice rode the long plains under shifting skies. He rode easily, rifle in hand, eyes narrowed as he searched the deceptively flat land. Water had cut deep coulees there at intervals, washes deep enough to conceal an army where it might be invisible to the casual searcher.

The timber and hills rose up ahead, offering more concealment for an enemy. The question in Ruff's mind was why the hostile Cheyenne would want to hide at all. They had the wagon train pretty much where they had wanted it—pinned down, out in the open. Lack of ammunition? Lack of numbers? Maybe they had struck the wagons as a target of opportunity but were needed more somewhere else. Stone Eyes wouldn't like it much if he had summoned all his forces and one band had taken it on its own to start an isolated battle . . . maybe.

There were no answers on the plains—and no visible Cheyenne. Until Ruff reached the timber.

There the lone Indian sat his feathered pony. He was an older warrior, wearing a feathered bonnet, dressed in elkskins. Ruff tensed, and the Indian lifted his hand in the sign for peace.

"Swamp Cheyenne," Justice said to himself, lowering his rifle to lift his own right hand.

When he rode nearer, he recognized the beadwork on the elkskins and thought he recognized the Indian's face.

"Ruff Justice."

"War Eagle," Justice responded. The Swamp Cheyenne thrust out his hand, and Ruff took it.

"You will not find them," the old warrior said.

"You know who I'm looking for?"

"Stone Eyes' warriors. They are gone, all gone." The Indian's arm stretched southward.

"You're sure?"

"Very sure," the Swamp Cheyenne answered.

"You saw them then."

"We saw it all. Not long ago, Justice, the army wanted to make a war with us. Not long ago we were chased from our home along the Flame."

"I recall it." Justice had been there.

"Not this time." The old man shook his head. "We will not have a war like this on our land. To the whites, Indian is Indian, Cheyenne is Cheyenne. They are gone—the Swamp Cheyenne told them to go. You will tell the army that? You will tell MacEnroe we are still at peace?"

"I'll tell him," Ruff promised.

War Eagle just nodded and turned his horse away. "Wait a minute," Justice said. "Have you seen a band of whites riding toward the town of Deadwater?"

"Small band? Ten men. With wounded." War Eagle's eyes were smiling though his mouth remained a straight line, carved into his mahogany face. "Someone told me that a man in buckskins shot some of them. I do not know who that could be. They are bad men, Ruff Justice?"

"They are."

"They mean trouble for my people?"

"No, I don't think so. It's something for us to solve, not you."

"Good," the old chief said, "I want no part of white man's wars no more."

Justice couldn't blame him for that. The Swamp Cheyenne had been beaten, shoved onto a reservation, pushed off again, lied to, and cheated.

"Thank you, War Eagle."

"I hope your enemies will soon be dead." The Cheyenne hesitated. "I ask you one thing—have you seen someone else? An Apache?"

"Apache?"

"You think I am mad or old, perhaps, but last night

a man came to our camp. A man like a shadow. This man took Iron Hand's best war pony. Took it while Iron Hand slept next to it with a tether from his hand to the horse's foot. The man left the tracks of an Apache. Once I met the Apache. I did not like them. I know Apache sign, though—this man was Apache."

"I've seen this sign, but not the man. I think he wants me," Ruff Justice said.

"In that case, be very careful, Justice. This one is good, very good indeed."

"I'll be careful. Tell Iron Hand I'll try to bring his war pony back to him."

"I hope you do not do that, Ruff Justice. You would not want to walk the trail he is walking. Iron Hand is dead. The same Apache killed him."

Then the Cheyenne lifted his hand again and rode off into the deep timber, leaving Justice to sit his spotted horse. He wondered what kind of a man he was up against—a man with the gall and the ability to walk into a Cheyenne camp, casually steal a horse, and coldly kill its owner.

The Apache was, as War Eagle had said, very good. And very deadly.

11

Ruff Justice found McCulloch riding at the head of the column of settlers, his injured arm in a sling. The wagon master watched Justice warily as he approached.

"It's clear up ahead," Justice told him, and McCulloch relaxed a little.

"Sure?"

"Quite sure." Justice told him briefly what had happened. "The Swamp Cheyenne didn't want trouble on their land. They ran them off."

"And you believe the Indian that told you that!"

"I believe it," Ruff said stiffly. "It's the truth. It doesn't mean we've got clear sailing, though. Dan Court is still ahead. War Eagle says he's got ten men left, enough to make trouble."

"He can try. The people on this wagon train aren't going to quit now, though. We've all been through a lot—too much to let someone like Dan Court run us off."

McCulloch was dead serious, his face more thoughtful than angry. It was one of the few moments when Justice could almost like the man.

He pulled off and let McCulloch ride on. The

wagon master's own wagon passed next, driven by a willowy young mother McCulloch had finally agreed to share with. Behind them came the Schoendienst wagon, with Taylor Cribbs driving, the two kids seated beside her.

" 'Morning, Ruff!" she called, "how's it look."

Ruff rode alongside, stepped onto the wagon bench, and took the reins. The kids, squealing and laughing, ducked into the back.

"How are they doing?" Justice asked, nodding toward the back of the covered wagon.

"The kids are all right. . . . I'm not sure about Mrs. Schoendienst. She spends a lot of time crying hard."

Justice nodded. "It'll be tough for her."

"She's never mentioned going back. Says her husband wanted to go West, so she's going."

"She'll pull through then."

"Think so?" Taylor cocked her head and smiled wistfully. "Think we'll all pull through?—or are we just rolling toward the end of the line?"

"I said you'll make it, damn you, Taylor Cribbs. It's a chance for a new life, whatever kind of life you want."

"People don't change easily, Ruff. Give them every opportunity, and they seem to prefer to stay the same."

"You too?" he asked.

She shrugged, her eyes turning away from his. Justice put his arm around her and guided the team with one hand. Schoendienst had had no idea how to drive oxen, and so he'd come up with a yoke and rein rig, not realizing that the oxen would go where they were pointed without much fuss.

"Will we make it tonight?" Taylor wanted to know. There was another question in her eyes.

"Not tonight. Tomorrow with luck."

"Good."

Ruff looked at her with interest. "You're not in a hurry now? Everyone else is."

"No, I'm in no hurry. Maybe I'm scared to see what the rest of my life might look like. Maybe I . . . just want to have one more night like we had back down the trail."

"Maybe," Ruff Justice said without much doubt, "we will do just that."

The little boy stuck his head out from behind the canvas. "What kinda night?" he asked.

Taylor laughed. "Never mind."

"You're gonna live with us in Deadwater. Momma said," the boy told her, climbing up on the bench seat. He had a toy rifle in his hand and sat studying the prairie and the hills ahead with serious eyes.

"Momma says," Taylor repeated, looking at Ruff. Her eyes were wistful and uncertain.

"That's a decision you can make later." Ruff turned to the boy and said, "What's the gun for?"

"Indians."

"There won't be any more Indians. You call tell your momma that too."

"No more Indians?" He looked crestfallen. "You're sure, Mr. Justice?"

"Sure as can be."

"Darn it. I hoped they'd come back."

"You did?" Taylor asked in surprise. "Why in the world would you hope that, Daniel?"

"I was going to kill the one that shot Daddy," he answered with utmost seriousness. "Kill him dead."

Ruff Justice said nothing. Taylor looked away. Another generation, Ruff thought. There were thousands of Indians out here who hated all whites—men like Stone Eyes—because someone had taken something from them, because their friends and family had been killed. And there were thousands of whites who hated Indians for the same reason. It wouldn't end soon. Some bitterness can last a lifetime; and prejudice is often passed down to the next generation as a kind of dark heritage.

Back East some of the new wave of thinkers—people who had never been shot at or seen women scalped and tortured—had decided that the whites were wrong because they had come to America, gone West. But that was the history of the world. People moved, other people were pushed. The weak move or are killed. Justice had no idea how you solved it. Send everyone home? He only hoped the savage, honorable Indian race didn't vanish.

One of the oxen stepped in a prairie dog hole and stumbled in surprise. It shook its massive head in confusion and walked on. The sun was setting now, and Ruff knew they would soon have to stop.

Night camp was in the pines. They could have seen the lights of Deadwater if there had been any lights to see. But Deadwater was still empty, waiting for people to bring it to life. Only Susan Donner and her cowhands lived there now, and they were five miles out of town to the south on the old ranch. Ruff stood on a flat, moss-covered outcropping looking toward Deadwater. He could hear and smell the Flame River, and he couldn't yet see it. Below, the camp, ragged and more cheerful now, sheltered the expectant settlers.

Taylor wasn't exactly silent as she walked upslope to where Justice stood, but she moved lightly and gracefully across the earth, as if she had shed some burden. She was a night creature, a vision in pale blue. Taylor stepped next to Ruff Justice, and for a time she too was silent, just watching, maybe trying to see into her own future.

"Is that it?" she asked at length.

"Deadwater? Yes. You can make out the corner of a building—the hotel maybe, on that ridge."

She peered intently for a long while. "I can't. You must have good eyes."

"Just experience. And I know where it is."

"You've been here before. I forget."

"Yes." There was something on her mind.

"You know this woman, this Susan Donner?"

"I know her," Justice replied.

"An older woman . . ."

"Twenty or so."

Taylor's mouth tightened a little. "You . . ." she began, but Ruff Justice cut her off.

"I know Susan Donner. She's a young woman and she's beautiful. I won't say attractive or pretty—she's downright beautiful. Once I knew her well. Now the only interest I have in her is an unhappy one. I have to give her the word that the man she was going to marry was killed by Indians while he was out on patrol. Mike Drew was his name, a hell of a man. She's been counting on Mike to help her set up the ranch and keep it going—counting on him to give her a shoulder, a strong hand to help her out. I have to tell her Mike won't be coming."

"Sorry, Justice."

"Why?" Ruff turned toward her, and his arms went around her waist, drawing her close. "Sorry because you're a little jealous? Nothing flatters a man more."

"More than a little jealous." She laughed. Her fingers stroked his jaw, tracing a route down his strong, tanned neck to his chest. Then she gripped his shirt front tightly, pulling his mouth to hers.

"Let's walk," Ruff said when she finally broke off the kiss.

They strode upward through the pines, arms around each other's waists, the cool air whispering secret words in the pines. They found a clearing deep in the forest and lay down as the moon, pale and nearly full, rose in the east.

Taylor slipped from her dress and lay soft and golden in the moonlight, her arms stretched out for Justice, who went to her, throwing his shirt aside.

"Forgot something," Taylor said as Ruff nuzzled her ear, listening to her rapid, fluttering breaths. He kissed her throat, the strong pulse there dancing beneath his lips.

"Did I?"

"These," Taylor said. Her hand ran up the leg of his buckskins to his crotch, where she cupped his swelling need.

"I guess I won't need them much," Ruff admitted.

Taylor found the strings and undid his trousers, tugging them down with effortful, pleased exclamations. Ruff reached around and toyed with her full breasts as she worked at removing his boots, getting his buckskin pants off.

"You're a big help," she whispered.

"I try."

"Want me to do it all?"

"Sounds like a good idea," Justice teased, wrapping his fingers in the hair at the nape of her neck, drawing himself close to her for one more lingering kiss, feeling the swipe of her tongue across his lips, the warm dampness of her mouth.

She pulled away breathlessly. "Tease. Damned tease . . ." The trousers were tugged off over his feet, and Justice lay naked on his back in the pine-ringed clearing, watching the taut, lovely body of the woman who now straddled him, facing away.

His hands went to her smooth, perfect buttocks and stroked them gently as Taylor reached for his thickening erection. She held it gently for a moment and then tucked it away in her warmth, settling on it. Her fingers stroked his shaft, making frequent expeditions down his tightening sack, wondering at his maleness.

Taylor leaned far forward and kissed Justice's feet as Ruff's fingers came from behind to join Taylor's, exploring her dampness, the tender outer perimeters of her body, finding his own shaft where it entered her. Taylor straightened then, throwing back her head and settling deeply onto Ruff as her body released a rush of fluid satisfaction.

Justice sat up, cupped her breasts, and bit at her sleek neck. She held his hands to her breasts, her taut pink nipples the focus of tingling sensation. Then she guided them to her thickly tufted crotch, joining Justice as he stroked the erect tab of flesh there.

"Justice . . ." she said from deep in her throat, and then she pulled away from him suddenly.

On hands and knees she reached back and spread herself as Justice, smiling softly in the pine-scented darkness, eased up behind her smooth, perfect buttocks and offered himself to the redhead.

She reached back, moaning distantly, found his solid erection, and guided it into her depths.

"Justice . . ." she said again dreamily. Her head was folded on her arms against the ground. The moon glossed her body. She quivered once and then collapsed as Justice continued to sway against her, driving deeply into her cleft.

He finished with a sudden, loin-shaking rush, and

Taylor trembled and lay still, Ruff on top of her, kissing her neck, her ear, her smooth back.

Justice slept deeply and long—it had been days since he had had a full night's sleep. When he woke up, yawning, the sun was a vast red presence in the eastern sky.

Taylor Cribbs, half-dressed, her hair in disarray, was standing over him, rifle in hand.

"Planning on shooting someone?"

"If I had to. Ruff, there was someone out here last night, watching us."

Justice sat up, scratching his head. "You're sure?"

"Very sure. I picked up your rifle. I was hoping I wouldn't have to fire it—it would probably break my shoulder. I don't know a lot about guns, but I know how to cock one and pull the trigger. I've . . ."

Her voice broke off. She didn't know much about guns, but she had known enough about them to have killed a would-be rapist once. Justice stood, pulled on his trousers, and took his .56 back.

"Who was he?"

"I don't know, Ruff. Maybe it was a dream, or just my imagination, but it seemed to me that someone was here." She turned toward him. "And it seemed to me he was an Apache Indian."

"Apache." Ruff was silent for a minute. Then he broke into a grin, hugging her, pulling Taylor to him to kiss her throat. "When have you seen an Apache Indian?"

"Never, but I've seen pictures. Maybe I'm crazy."

Maybe. Maybe Justice was going crazy as well. But he knew there was an Apache out there, a deadly one. And he knew the only reason he hadn't gotten his throat cut like Iron Hand had was because a loving, caring woman had been standing watch with his big buffalo gun.

"I'll walk you back to the camp," Justice said.

"Today?" She asked, almost in disbelief. "We'll reach Deadwater?"

"Today," Ruff promised her. Today they would reach Deadwater, and Susan Donner would have to receive the bad news. Today they would reach Deadwater where Dan Court presumably waited to wipe out the settlers, steal their goods, and take over the town.

Deadwater—where the Apache, whoever he was, waited.

"Come on," Justice said, "let's roll. Let's finish it." But the finish was a long way off, and Justice knew it. Ahead of them lay only trouble, more trouble. More blood.

12

Deadwater lay empty, gray, and still in the morning light as the wagon train rolled up its rutted, brush-clotted street.

It still wasn't much of a town. Gray unpainted buildings, their porches falling down, morosely watched the travelers arriving in their overloaded wagons. To Justice and his charges it was earthly paradise.

"Well, you got us here," McCulloch said to Justice. Even the wagon master was in a good mood this morning.

"Not a day too soon," Justice answered. He'd had enough of this band of settlers, with the exception of Taylor Cribbs. He wanted to rest his horse, grab a meal, and ride back to Lincoln, where every soldier took care of himself. Each man knew his duties and performed them as well as possible, with a minimum of bickering.

But it wasn't going to be that easy. There was still Susan Donner, there was still Dan Court.

And there was still the Apache.

"Where's the hardware store? That it?" McCulloch shouted.

Ruff nodded. McCulloch beamed. The hardware

store was his by default. He was the only one who could claim it, the only one with stock.

The other buildings had multiple claimants. Three different men so far wanted the hotel—well, that was their problem, or Susan Donner's.

The wagons halted. For a long time people just sat in the middle of the street, gazing in wonder or exultation at the empty town. Susan Donner's father had built it on speculation when he discovered that the railroad would be coming through. A town born, expired, and now about to rise from the grave.

"Ought to rename it Phoenix," Justice said.

"How's that?" Tom Beers asked.

"Never mind. You want to go straight on through to the Donner ranch with me?"

"Me and Slick," Beers said, nodding at his remaining partner. "Sure. I don't care to see this town until they've opened the saloons."

Justice turned in his saddle, resting a hand on the spotted horse's back. "One minute," he said.

He rode to where Taylor Cribbs and Mrs. Schoendienst stood staring blankly at the empty streets. "I'm going down to the Donner ranch, Taylor."

"Oh?" Was there a spark of jealousy in her green eyes?

"I imagine Susan will want to ride on down here and meet everyone, try to organize things. . . . First I've got to tell her about Mike Drew. Beers and Slick are going over to sign up as cowhands."

"What do we do, Mr. Justice?" Mrs. Schoendienst asked. She was holding her little girl, stroking her hair. The wind kicked up a tiny dust devil, which spun and danced down the street, they all turned briefly away.

"Wait and talk to Susan. For the time being, maybe

116

the best thing is to lay claim to a hotel room and get some real rest."

"Have they got real beds?" the little girl asked.

Justice smiled. "Last time I was here they did. You'll have to do a little cleaning up first, I'd imagine, but yes, they have real beds."

"About ready, Justice?" Tom Beers called.

"Just about—afraid of someone beating you to the job?"

"No, I guess not." Beers was rolling a cigarette. "Not too much competition around, is there?"

"I've got to go, Taylor. I'll be back tonight. We'll discuss things."

"All sorts of things?" she asked hopefully.

"We'll see. Stick with Mrs. Schoendienst and the kids for now, all right?"

"Sure," she said. There was resignation in her voice as she looked toward the saloon where two men now stood laughing with Dolly. "Dolly knows," Taylor said under her breath, but Justice heard her.

"Dolly doesn't know. Dolly just lacks imagination and confidence."

"Sure," Taylor answered without much enthusiasm. She half turned away, and when she looked back, Ruff Justice was riding out of town with Beers and Slick.

"What on earth were you talking about?" Mrs. Schoendienst asked, looking from the saloon to Justice and back.

"Nothing. Imagination. Come on, kids!" Taylor said brightly. "Let's see if we can't find a room for us in the hotel."

Tom Beers smoked silently. Slick rode with his head down, exhausted. Justice looked at the river which ran toward the Donner ranch, then at the pines and long grass valley.

"What's the matter with the redhead?" Tom Beers asked finally, flipping his dead cigarette away.

"She doesn't like what she is, but she's afraid to change," Justice answered.

"Oh." Beers was thoughtful for a minute. "I guess I can understand that. Don't want to be a saloon girl, is that it?"

"That's it."

Slick spoke up. "Hell, I known a lot of 'em took off and married some cowboy or even a banker. In this country people got the *right* to change."

Yes, and Taylor Cribbs ought to realize that. They began to see cattle—not good stuff yet, mostly longhorns, Mexican beef—but if Susan could come by a good bull, she had the grass and the water, the opportunity. Susan had wanted to change; she had made herself into a rancher.

They spotted two ranch hands, both Mexican vaqueros, and drifted toward them. The dark faces watched with some mistrust. Their hands weren't far from their holstered pistols as Justice and the two Texans approached.

"Buenas tardes," Ruff said. "The name's Ruff Justice. Is Señorita Donner at the ranch house?"

"Yes," one of the vaqueros said in heavily accented English. "Ruff Justice—I think I hear this name from la señorita."

"This is Tom Beers. This is Slick. They plan on working for Señorita Donner."

"I am Miguel Andojar. *Mi compadre*, Esteban," he said, nodding toward the other vaquero.

"You drove these cattle up from down south?"

"Part way. From Colorado. A long, long drive,"

118

Andojar said. "We are short of men, very short. We would be happy to have you with us, even," he said with a bright smile, "if you are from Tejas."

Beers grinned and offered his hand. Esteban took it and then Miguel Andojar. "The lady," Andojar said, "is at the big house."

"We'll get on down there," Ruff said. "Tell me, has there been any trouble around here?"

"Trouble? *Indios?*"

"Them, too; we got hit by some hostiles a way back, but I was thinking of some whites. Raiders. Don't know exactly what they have in mind."

"No, Ruff Justice, nothing like that. Only one thing . . ." Andojar shrugged as if it were of no importance.

"What thing is that?" he prodded.

"The other night I saw something—maybe a dream, eh? It made no sense."

"What was it?"

"Nothing. A crazy dream, I think. But I saw a woman, an old woman all in black riding alone through the pines. But no woman came to the house; no woman was seen by anyone else. A dream, Ruff Justice. What would an old woman be doing out here alone? Where would she have come from?"

"Do you have dreams like that often?" Justice asked.

Miguel smiled. "No, señor. I dream of young women, yes, but not like this. I saw her, but I do not understand it."

When they continued on, Beers asked Justice, "What was that business with you and the Mex? You knew what he was talking about, didn't you? I saw it in your eyes."

"Maybe," Justice said. "Maybe I know what he was talking about, Tom."

The ranch came suddenly into view. Everything was being rebuilt. Donner had been burned out, and the main house was slowly being put back together. Green lumber framing projected from the side of the house. The roof was still smoked, the white paint charred. The corral beneath the oaks was new, constructed with split rail. Two shirtless men were pounding nails at the site of a new barn.

"This'll be something," Slick said. "One day this'll be a real ranch." Coming from a Texan it was a large compliment.

Susan came out of the house, bucket in hand. She dumped a bucket of water and then stood with one hand on her hip, watching the incoming riders. Then she recognized one of them, or thought she did. Susan Donner dropped the bucket then, half running forward into the hard-packed yard.

"Ruff Justice!" she called, and Justice grinned.

Susan was a compact, well-made woman with copper hair and a small, pleasant mouth. She wore brown checked gingham and an expression that was warm and amused.

Justice waved, his smile slowly fading. He had nearly forgotten why he had come. To crush her heart.

The three men rode into the yard, and Ruff swung down to be engulfed in an embrace. She pulled back, looked into his eyes, and hugged him again.

Then she looked up at Beers and Slick and asked, "You brought me some help—I hope?"

Ruff introduced the two men, and Susan said, "You fellows ready to get to work right away?"

"Yes, miss. If you need us."

"I need you, all right. I could use a dozen more. Go on over to the bunkhouse—that's it beyond the oaks—

get yourselves something to eat, and then change horses. Take your pick from the corral—anyone but the blue roan, that's mine, then find my foreman. Miguel is—"

"We met Miguel. I know where he is," Tom said.

"Good. We've got some stock lost up along Grand Peak. Cougar spooked 'em, killed two calves—didn't eat 'em, just killed 'em. Find that cougar, and there's twenty extra dollars for you. Oh," she said, "I pay a dollar a day and found. No whisky in the bunkhouse."

"Yes, miss," Tom Beers said, touching his hat brim. He winked at Justice, turned his horse, and rode toward the bunkhouse with Slick following him.

"They good men, Ruffin?"

"The best."

"Well . . ." She looked him over again. "Come in, come on into the house such as it is and have some cool lemonade. Tell me what brings you out this way."

She slipped her arm around Ruff's waist and walked him back toward the porch.

"I've brought you your town, Susan."

She stopped. "You don't mean it?"

"I do. We rolled into Deadwater not an hour ago. A banker, a hardware merchant, some hotel keepers, family men . . ."

"And women? Jesus, Ruff, I haven't seen a person of my own sex since . . . what is it?" she asked, growing suddenly subdued. There was something in Justice's eyes . . . "God, it's Mike," she said.

"It's Mike. Want to go inside and sit down?"

"No, damn it, Ruffin! I want to know. Now!"

"He's dead. Indians. He was on a patrol chasing Stone Eyes. Mike won't be back."

Her eyes were blank. She had gone hollow; she spoke from far away. "I knew it. Do you understand that? A few nights ago I woke up with an ache inside me. I knew it. God, Ruffin, what a life we live. Come on in, rest."

She did it very well. She was polite and gracious as she poured lemonade in the small half-furnished parlor, but the tears sprang up suddenly, and she couldn't stop them from falling.

"Excuse me, Ruffin," she said. Then she turned and stumbled to an inner room.

Justice sat sipping his bitter lemonade, watching a mockingbird on the windowsill. It was a long time before Susan emerged, but she had gained control of herself. It was a hard land, but she was a strong woman. She had fought like hell for this ranch, for the town. She had seen her mother die on the Flame River. Now she had lost the man she had counted on marrying. But she held her feelings back. Only her red-rimmed eyes betrayed her.

"Sorry, Ruffin. More lemonade—something to eat?"

"I could eat something."

"There's a cold roast. Some cheese—probably not very good. I've just started learning how to make it."

"Sounds good."

She went away again into the kitchen, and only once did Ruff hear the frustrated, angry sound of something metal being thrown to the floor.

The cheese wasn't that good, but it was filling, and the cold rare roast excellent. Susan changed into a dark green riding skirt and jacket while Ruff ate. When she returned to the room, she looked fresh and fit.

"I'm ready," she said. "Let's go meet these townspeople you've brought me, Ruff Justice. If I can't have anything else, at least I'll have my town."

Once, long ago, they had made love among the pines, and Ruff knew her statement was also a question, an expression of regret. She had lost Mike Drew, and she knew she couldn't have Justice. Or could she? Ruff shook his head and rose, reaching for his hat. He tried to ignore all the implications of her searching, tired eyes.

"Let's see what we can do about making Deadwater a town again."

"Justice . . . oh, damn it all. . . ."

Then Susan stalked from the room, slapping her leg with her riding quirt. Very efficient and self-reliant, she only stumbled once before reaching the door.

They caught up the blue roan, saddled it, and rode northward again toward Deadwater.

They got there just in time to stop the raging riot.

13

＊＊＊＊ ━━◆━━ ＊＊＊＊

Deadwater was in chaos. A fistfight was in progress in front of the hotel; two middle-aged men in torn shirts were going at it to beat the band. As Ruff pointed them out to Susan Donner, they hit the ground together, rolling off the plank walk and into the street. Someone threw a chair from an upstairs window. An armed man stood guard in front of the dry goods store as a small crowd of people carrying crates tried to force their way past him.

Farther up the street, an overturned wagon had been set on fire, and yet another fight was taking place, perilously close to the flames. A woman was screaming, pulling at the hair and clothes of one of the men. Somewhere an unidentifiable crash sounded, followed by a loud string of curses.

"What in blazes are they doing to my town!" Susan Donner cried. She unsheathed her Winchester and put four rounds into the air. The brawling stopped, and the men scrambled to their feet.

"That's better," Susan said, walking her horse forward.

"Who in hell are you, lady?" a thick man with bushy black eyebrows asked. His name was Tinker, and he was one of the three who had hoped to run the hotel in Deadwater.

"I'm Susan Donner. This is my property you're on, my property you're tearing up. What's the matter with you, the bunch of you?"

They watched her as she spoke, but no one looked especially ashamed. Grinning, Ortega sauntered up to Justice.

"What happened, Felipe?" Ruff asked.

Justice swung down from his horse and helped Susan down from her blue roan. Felipe told him what he knew. "I was at the stable when Tinker and Gadsen got into it first, but I came out to watch. It beat shoveling manure."

Ruff and Susan had stepped up onto the plank walk in front of the hotel. A crowd was slowly forming now that people realized who Susan was. It was a bloody, fire-smoked, ragged crowd. Minutes ago it had been a mob. They were desperate and a little frightened; they had come a long way for a piece of this pie, and they wanted it. Now.

Felipe went on, "Tinker started moving his gear into the hotel office, and Gadsen told him to stop. It didn't take long for them to go to fists."

"What about the other fights?" Susan asked, glancing at the crowd.

"Same thing. People were standing around, waiting. McCulloch—he was our wagon master—started moving his goods into the hardware store. He's the only one wanted that or had the goods to operate it. Other people started getting antsy. Afraid that someone else would beat them to their ambition. Down the street Max Cord and Harry Green looked at each other and made a mad dash for the general store. That ended up with Green and his son spilling Cord's wagon and setting fire to it so Cord wouldn't have any goods to sell.

"On the whole, amigo, it was not a pretty scene."

Ruff nodded. It reminded him of a land rush or a rush to stake out gold claims. He half understood it—these people had come a long way, and most of them had no place to return to if they failed here. They were willing to fight for what they thought should be theirs.

But Susan wasn't willing to let that happen.

"No one," she told the crowd, "owns anything yet. No one but me. Try to take something by force, and you'll never get anything."

"I was in the building first," Harry Green shouted.

"I don't care if you were there three years before anyone else," Susan shot back. "This is my town. That's my store, this is my hotel."

"What about those promises in the newspaper advertisement?" Cord shouted. He was a small, red-faced man—now nearly purple from the excitement and his fight with Green.

"What about them? I asked for citizens for Dead-water, and I promised you a livelihood."

"And you choose who gets to have what."

"That's right," Susan snapped. Ruff grinned. He was proud of her. It hadn't been an easy morning for Susan Donner, but she was handling this well.

"What I have in mind," she announced, "is a lottery. We'll rig up something—maybe use the saloon roulette wheel or draw numbers. If you want some good advice, however, you'll figure this out beforehand for yourselves."

"What do you mean?" Green asked.

"Just this—people have gone into business together before. Why not have a Cord-Green general store? If you can agree to that before we draw names, neither of you will have to worry about losing."

Tinker said, "Yeah, but I never heard of three men running a hotel."

"There are other options," Susan insisted. "There's an empty building down the block which was never used for anything. It could be whatever you wanted. A saddlery, a clothing store, anything at all!"

"So someone else gets the hotel complete with beds and furniture, and I get an empty building when I haven't got the goods to fill it up."

"All I'm offering," Susan said stiffly, "is a chance. The railroad's going to be coming through here in the next six months, and when it does, everyone will prosper."

"What do I do until then?" Tinker demanded.

Susan was a lady; she refrained from answering his question. "The lottery is tonight at the saloon across the street. Until then, take your belongings out of these buildings and go back into your wagons."

"Lady," a narrow man with a thin mustache called Blodgett said, "it's going to be a hell of a saloon meeting if I have to take my whisky barrels back out."

Blodgett could afford to joke. Deadwater had three saloons, and so far only he and Joe Connely intended to set up as saloonkeepers.

"Roll them out anyway," Susan said.

"What about people sleeping in the hotel?"

Susan turned toward the tall, redheaded woman who stood in the doorway behind her. Green-eyed and beautiful, she looked briefly across Susan's shoulder at Ruff Justice. Susan caught the look.

"Stay where you are," she told Taylor.

"Thank you. Thank you very much," Taylor Cribbs

said dryly. Then she turned and went into the hotel, closing the door solidly.

"Yours?" Susan Donner asked. "No, Never mind. It must be yours, Ruffin T. Justice."

"I make friends easily."

"I know. All the best types."

"We'd better talk privately, Susan," Justice suggested. People had begun to drift away in twos and threes.

"About that?" She nodded toward the hotel door.

"No, not about her. About Deadwater."

"All right." She nodded. "The restaurant?"

"Sure."

It was next door to the hotel—a dusty, empty building guarded by a buxom matron with folded arms. "No one else wants the restaurant, do they?" the woman asked beseechingly. "If I can't have it, I don't know what'll become of me."

Susan was short with her. "We'll find out tonight."

The woman exploded. "*You* brought us out here. You and your advertisement. You dragged us through hard weather and an Indian fight—my husband was killed! You owe us!"

Susan's mouth tightened, but she didn't answer. She opened the restaurant door and went in, followed by Ruff Justice.

Susan Donner dusted off a chair as best she could and sat, briefly burying her face in her hands. She wasn't crying; she was only weary.

"This is a great start, isn't it, Ruff? That was a hell of a good idea I had, advertising for citizens. And what a bunch they are!"

"They're all right, most of them. They're just tired and scared. Things will settle down."

"They will, will they?—then what did you bring me over here for, Ruff? Tell me that."

Ruff broke into a grin. "You know me pretty well, don't you, Susan?"

"Well enough to know when you're trying to bolster someone's sagging confidence. What did you want to tell me?"

"More of the same. Men like Green and Cord aren't going to be reasonable about this. Tinker has blood in his eyes as well. If they don't get what they want, I've an idea they'll try to take it."

"And. . . ? There's something else."

"There's something else," Ruff Justice admitted. "A raider named Dan Court has been dogging this wagon train. I think the only reason he didn't loot it was because there were hostile Indians around. He was waiting his turn."

"And now his turn has come."

"I think so. Soon, anyway. He's got ten men, all willing to do whatever they have to do. I think he'll want to hit Deadwater while everything is still crated up—easy to move and sell—but he may plan on taking the whole town."

"I see." Susan was thoughtful.

"I brought you all kinds of trouble, didn't I?"

"Trouble comes," she said philosophically.

"Right now these people aren't ready to fight. They'll have to be made ready. Everyone with a rifle ready, a post to go to in case of more trouble, a place to stash the kids. You're going to have to help them. The first thing you ought to do is have an election for a mayor and town council.

"Then find yourself a town marshal, because you're going to need one," Justice said soberly.

"Any suggestions for mayor?"

"Can't think of anyone but Felipe Ortega, and I doubt they'd vote him in."

"Then they can have whoever they want." Susan tugged nervously at her hair. Then she smiled. "I know who I want for town marshal, though. . . . Sorry I don't have a badge for you."

"Forget that," Justice said. "I'm no lawman."

"Going to leave us to Dan Court, are you, Justice? Going to let those greedy sons of bitches tear down my town?"

"Quit smiling."

"I asked you a question."

"I work for the army," he grumbled. "I've done my job. I brought them here."

"And what would Colonel MacEnroe want you to do if he were here?"

"I asked you to quit smiling, Susan Donner."

"Maybe someone can cut a badge out of tin."

"Maybe someone could snip your ears off with some tin shears. I can't do it, Susan. I won't."

"No? I know you, Ruff Justice. You don't want to do it, but you will. Just until everything's settled. Until people are in their homes and businesses and this Dan Court is out of the territory. Or buried."

"Susan . . ."

"I know you'll do that much for me, for these people."

"Damn it, Susan," Ruff Justice said, "quit smiling."

She did, for a minute. "I've got a ranch to run, Ruffin. Want to come down and stay for a while?"

"What I want to do is get some sleep," Ruff answered.

"She keep you awake nights?" Susan Donner asked slyly.

"It's been a long trip out. I'll sack out in the hotel."

"Oh." Susan pursed her lips and tilted her head. "I see. Eight o'clock tonight. We'll have that meeting in the saloon and see what kind of fireworks we can set off."

Ruff walked her out to the street and stood for a minute watching Deadwater. People clustered together in patches of shade beneath awnings, beside buildings, and waited.

"I almost liked it better empty," Susan Donner said.

"It'll all heal."

"Sure." She swung aboard her blue roan. "I'll be seeing you, marshal."

Ruff grinned and lifted a hand in farewell. He watched Susan ride away, then turned and tramped into the hotel.

Empty and musty, the hotel rang with the shouts of the two Schoendienst kids. Taylor stood at the foot of the stairs, waiting.

"Took you awhile to get rid of her."

"There's a lot to straighten out."

"Uh-huh," she said.

"You might start passing the word that the lottery's at eight o'clock tonight."

"All right."

Ruff tilted her chin up and kissed her. "Don't sulk, it's not appealing."

"I suppose you're going to sleep?"

"I'm going to try. Any of the rooms halfway decent?"

"They're all right. Try the one to the right at the top of the stairs. No, wait, the one on the left. The old woman took the other one."

Ruff turned slowly, his eyes narrowing. "What old woman? You mean Mary Caffiter?"

"No, not her. A woman I never saw before. Little hunched thing all dressed in black, wearing a veil."

"And black gloves."

"Sure, but . . . what is it, Ruff?" Taylor asked with concern. "Your face—"

"What room did you say she was in?"

"On the right, the head of the stairs. But, why, Ruff?"

"I just want to see her and talk to her."

"She's probably sleeping, too."

"She'll wake up then," Justice said, looking toward the landing.

"I don't understand you; what's the matter?"

"I'm not sure. Something I haven't figured out yet. Where in hell did this woman come from?"

"Why, I don't know. She was just here."

"Rode all this way alone, past the Indians."

"I thought maybe she was from around here," Taylor said. Ruff had started up the stairs, and she scrambled after him.

"Stay down there," he said sharply.

"Why? What in hell is this, Justice?"

"Stay there," he repeated, but Taylor Cribbs stayed on his heels as he mounted the stairs and rapped sharply at the door on the right.

"She's sleeping, Justice."

"I'm opening the door, Taylor."

"Just hold your horses! Have you gone crazy? Listen, I'll peek in, all right? You'll scare her half to death the way you look."

"Just open the door."

Taylor turned the oval-shaped brass knob, and the door swung in on rusty hinges. Ruff pulled her to one side of the doorway and drew his Colt revolver.

"Justice!" Taylor shrieked in frustration, but Ruff

didn't pay any attention. He cocked his Colt and stepped into the empty room.

"Gone!" Taylor said. "When do you suppose . . . ?"

Her eyes lifted to the open window across the room. The breeze pushed and tugged at the yellow curtain. Justice went to the window and peered down. He saw a ledge and then a stack of empty barrels.

"She's gone." Taylor glanced around the room. "What is going on here, Justice? Who is she?"

"I don't know," Ruff answered, holstering his Colt as he stood at the window, staring out at the back alley. "I don't know, but I mean to find out."

"It's someone," Taylor Cribbs said nervously, "that you want to kill, isn't it?"

Ruff turned slowly toward her. His voice was grim. "I don't want to kill anyone, Taylor. But it looks very much like the lady in black wants to kill me. Badly."

"What are you going to do now?"

"Now?" Ruff smiled and glanced at the bed. "Now I'm going to sleep. This room's empty, isn't it?"

"Justice . . ." But there was no talking to the man. Ruff stretched out on the bed, folded his arms, and was asleep in minutes. There was nothing for Taylor Cribbs to do but slip quietly out of the room, closing the door behind her.

14

At sundown Ruff Justice opened his eyes and lay there, looking around the unfamiliar room until he was fully alert. The window behind him was still open, and the night breeze, cooler by far, gusted through the room.

It was time to get up, but he didn't rise immediately. Something was nagging at the back of his mind, and it took him awhile to identify it.

The dream.

The dream was what had awakened him—not the knowledge that Susan and her town were going to be making some important determinations soon, and he wanted to be there.

It was the dream.

The dream: a hundred little old ladies in black wearing feathered warbonnets were attacking the wagon train Ruff was leading. All of the wagons had only two wheels, like ox carts. All of them were filled with old women in black.

Somehow the world caught on fire, and the Conklin brothers were screaming and racing around in circles, becoming old women in black. Then they were Apaches, with blue-black hair and razor-thin eyes.

One of them shot an arrow at Justice, but he managed to snatch it out of the air. It immediately turned into a crushed bird, and Justice let it drop.

The old lady beside him was suddenly Taylor Cribbs, and she said, "See, I told you you can't change."

There might have been more to the dream, but that was all Justice could recall. He shook his head, smiling at his own mind's creation, and rolled to the side of the bed, swinging his feet to the floor.

Justice left the room. The hallway was nearly dark, with only a dully glowing lamp lit on the landing. There seemed to be no one around, so Justice slipped downstairs and went out, using the door at the back of the empty kitchen.

Someone had been trying to do some cooking there. The smell of beef stew, tomatoes, and black pepper hung in the air, reminding Justice that he hadn't had a good meal for a hell of a long time.

Outside it was still, the sky bright with stars. He paused outside the door, looking up and down the alley, seeing nothing.

But he *felt* something, some presence—soft and wispy, deadly and cold.

Or maybe it was only an echo of the dream. Justice tugged his hat down and started up the alley. His boots were nearly silent against the red clay earth. He could hear nothing anywhere in the town.

"I know you're out there, Dan Court," Justice muttered in the darkness. "What are you waiting for?"

"Say something, amigo?" Felipe Ortega asked from out of the night.

The Mexican had a gun in his hands. He shrugged. "I have not forgotten Dan Court either. I have little, but now I have a place of my own—the stable. I will keep it."

"Damned horse," Ruff mumbled. The fog of sleep hadn't quite cleared away yet.

"What?"

"Forgot to stable up my horse," Justice told the Mexican hostler.

"I put him away long ago," Ortega said. "Rubbed down the spotted horse, gave it hay, and put salve on the wound on its neck. A bullet wound, I think?"

"Thanks, Felipe. You're a good man."

"Maybe," he shrugged. "Tell that to my wife in Durango. She thinks I am the devil's son. But I try to do my work right."

"I owe you."

"*Por nada.*"

Ruff Justice fished in his pocket and handed Ortega three double eagles. The Mexican stared at the gold coins. "I can't take this. Sixty dollars!"

"Take it and buy yourself some grain when you can. A few tools."

"For taking care of your horse? Ruff Justice, you are a madman with money."

"It was a sort of inheritance," Justice said. "I don't feel right about keeping it."

"There is blood on this money," Felipe said, understanding Justice now.

"Just a little bit of blood."

"Gold should have sweat on it, much sweat," Ortega told him, "but never blood."

"Keep it, use it. The blood's got nothing to do with you, Felipe."

Reluctantly Ortega pocketed the gold. "Dan Court?" he asked. "When will he come?"

"Soon. It'll have to be soon."

"Yes, I think so too. You are walking the town. Do you want help?"

"I wouldn't mind it. If Court comes, I think it'll be at night. There aren't too many people I can count on here. I wish Beers and Slick were still around to help out."

"I will watch. But Justice . . . will the others fight for this town if we must? Will they help us at all?"

"I don't know," Justice said. "Maybe not. Right now they're too busy fighting with one another. I'll try to talk to them tonight at the saloon."

"Then," Ortega said. "That is the time for Dan Court to attack us, while we're all in the same building, arguing among ourselves."

"That's the time. Maybe you'd better not show up, Felipe. Maybe you'd better find a good vantage point and watch. You see anything at all, fire that scattergun in the air. I'll watch out for your interests."

"I know you will, Justice. Tell me—all this effort, is it worth something?"

"If you want to have something, it is. You can't wait for the sky to open up and rain pesos. If you want something, you've got to work for it—fight for it. Sometimes you've got to die for it."

"Yes," Felipe said quietly. "You fight"—he brightened—"but die, I hope not!"

"I know," Justice said. "I've got to get going."

"Walk softly, Justice. I think the wolves are out."

"I think you're right. Walk softly yourself, Felipe."

Felipe smiled again and then slipped off into the night. Ruff Justice walked on, keeping to the shadows. The stars were bright and hard; a pale moon was rising. A few clouds cluttered the sky, and the wind was chilly.

Ruff circled the town, moving as if he were in

Indian country. Now and then he paused just to listen, to watch the seemingly empty land around Deadwater.

He went behind the general store—the store Green and Max Cord were ready to kill each other over. Crouched down, rifle across his knees, he watched and waited . . . waited for what?

Soon it would be time to walk over to the saloon and try to oversee the partitioning of Deadwater. Ruff rose and stretched, and the knife whipped through the air to embed itself in the wall of the general store, pinning his sleeve to the building.

Justice yanked his arm free and hit the ground. The Spencer came up, its shifting muzzle looking for a target, but nothing moved out there. There was nothing but the wind, and once a shadow, which Ruff was sure had been cast by a wind-propelled cloud. No man could move that silently, that quickly.

No human being.

Ruff stood, dusted himself off, and returned to the wall. He yanked the rawhide-handled knife from the building and weighed it in his hand for a moment.

"But shadows don't throw knives, do they, Justice?" he said to the night.

Not Apache knives.

By the time Justice returned to the main street of Deadwater and made his way toward the saloon—with Red Dog painted in faded letters on its facade—all of the town's would-be citizens had gathered outside on the porch, or inside at the dusty tables.

Their moods varied widely; there were the ebullient ones, who had assured themselves of a place of business or a home—McCulloch had already broken out a dark blue town suit—and the wary and sullen ones, who had to take their chances on the spin of a wheel or the luck of the draw. Tinker, Gadsen, O'Hara—all three wanted the hotel. Max Cord and Harry Green had still refused to compromise and go in as partners on the general store.

Ruff Justice almost walked past Harry Green before he turned suddenly, reaching his hand around the man. From inside Green's coat, Justice slipped the Remington pistol.

"You won't need that tonight," Justice said.

Green's red face was dark with anger. "That's just in case Dan Court shows up."

"If Dan Court shows up, you can ask for it back," Justice said, tucking the pistol behind his belt.

"What gives you the right . . . ?"

"Me," Ruff Justice smiled. "I'm the law here, or haven't you heard, Green?"

"I've heard. You've been bullying the bunch of us since Bismarck, and now you've got the idea in your head that you're going to keep on doing it here. One day, Justice, someone will take you down a notch."

"You?" Ruff asked mildly, but the shorter man could see something in the scout's ice-blue eyes. Something he knew he wasn't man enough to face up to. "Come on," Justice said, "let's go inside."

Green spun and stormed away, his boot heels pounding against the planks of the porch.

"He'll do something crazy if he doesn't win," Taylor Cribbs said. She wore a dark brown dress and shawl; her hair was pinned up at the nape of her neck. "Why don't you pull out, Ruff?"

"Don't want me around?"

"You don't belong here. It's not your town, not your dream. The people don't want you here."

"Not many of them."

"It's because you're an outsider. Because you're a

witness to their greed and hate. If Green or someone else wants to take out his anger on someone, it'll likely be you they'll look for."

"I imagine you're right."

"Why stay then? . . . Is it this Susan Donner?"

"Maybe it's because of you, Taylor."

"I doubt that," she said slowly, quietly.

"Maybe it's because I started something and I want to see it finished."

"Even," she said, "if it kills you."

McCulloch stuck his head out of the saloon door before Justice could answer. "Come on, folks," the wagon master said. "It's time to get started."

Inside, it was silent. People sat in the corners alone or clustered together around the tables. Susan Donner stood behind the long puncheon bar of the Red Dog with a brass bowl before her.

She glanced at Justice and Taylor Cribbs, her expression unreadable.

"Marshal," she said, "did you want to say a few words first?"

Ruff nodded and crossed the room, all eyes on him. He spoke simply. "Dan Court is likely still around. I want you all to figure out what you're going to do with your kids if he hits us. After you get settled, find a vantage place—if you got upstairs windows, those are the best—leave a rifle beside it and a box of dry cartridges."

"He won't try to take the whole town," Connely said.

"No? Want to gamble your life on it? But he *won't* take it if you people back one another up, watch out for your neighbor, and are willing to fight for Deadwater. You've come a long way and been through a lot. Don't give it away now."

"Is that all?" Green demanded harshly.

"Not quite. We need to have an election here. A show of hands will do. You need a mayor, and you need a town marshal. I've only got the job as marshal on an interim basis. You'll be rid of me soon enough."

"None too soon," someone muttered.

"None too soon."

"How about McCulloch for mayor," Tinker suggested.

"What do you care who's mayor? You'll be packing up soon enough," O'Hara said. The two would-be hotel owners glared at each other for a minute.

"That's not helping any," Susan Donner said. "I hear McCulloch—anyone else?"

No one was willing to nominate another man. McCulloch, beaming, was voted in in no time.

"For marshal?" Susan Donner asked.

"Felipe Ortega," Ruff Justice said.

"A greaser? Besides, you shouldn't have the right to nominate anyone. You don't live here."

"All right," Justice answered. "I'll withdraw the nomination. With a few remarks. Ortega is an upright, hardworking man with gumption and a knowledge of guns. Which one of you is willing to take on the job of handling Saturday night drunks, breaking up knife fights, laying your life on the line? You're merchants and saloonkeepers. If you've got a better man in mind, let's hear his name."

McCulloch surprised Justice again. He still hadn't figured out whether he liked the man or not; likely he never would. "I nominate Felipe Ortega," the new mayor said, "if he'll have the job."

Susan asked, "Other nominations?"

The townspeople looked at each other. No one at all

came to mind. Susan told them, "Looks like Ortega is your man."

"All right," Green shouted, "now let's get to what we came here for."

"All right." Susan leaned against the counter and looked out at the people in the saloon. "First, have any of you decided to take the reasonable way out of this? Mr. Green?"

"Share with Max Cord? Not likely."

"Gadsen?"

"I can't see three men running a hotel."

"And you don't want to try something else."

"Draw, lady, then we'll see."

Susan's mouth tightened a little. "All right. Let's do just that. I've put your names in this bowl. The first name drawn will have first choice of property. I've thrown out a few names. No one but Ortega wanted the stable, is that right?" Silence answered that question. "Only McCulloch for the hardware store? Only Mary Caffiter for the millinery shop?"

No one spoke up in opposition. Susan went on. "There's a little house east of town. The white one. I've taken that out of the drawing." There was a little grumbling at that; homes were going to be at a premium. "I'm giving it to Mrs. Schoendienst. She's a widow with two children, and to my way of thinking she needs it more than any of you."

"Thank you," the Schoendienst woman said. Her voice was choked.

Susan hesitated. It was time for the trouble. One in three of the rest of them would be pleased. The other two would be killing mad.

She drew a name. "Connely?"

"Right here."

"What'll it be."

"I like it fine where I am. The Red Dog suits me fine."

Susan nodded. "Mr. Blodgett, I suppose that gives you a choice of the other two saloons."

"Across the street," Blodgett said. "I'll take that one."

That was the easy part. The next draw was going to explode, and Susan knew it. Everyone knew it. "Max Cord," Susan Donner said.

"The general store," Cord said. He was leaning back in his chair, thumbs hooked in his belt loops. "That'll suit me just fine."

"Like hell!" Harry Green leapt to his feet. "I didn't come all this way for nothing." Ruff had under-estimated the man. He had taken one gun from Green, but now another one appeared miraculously in his hand. He swung around, firing at Max Cord, the bullet grooving the round table where his rival sat, scattering long splinters. "It's mine or it's no one's," Green shouted.

He was in a blind rage, quivering and slurring his words. He brought his pistol up again as men began to back toward the walls of the saloon.

"I'll kill you," Green said, but before he could do that, the blast of a shotgun from outside froze the motion of every man in that saloon.

"Ortega," Ruff Justice said. "Dan Court's coming in."

15

Justice moved with the first shot—not toward the front door, but toward the rear of the Red Dog. "Don't go out the front," he warned. But someone— Tinker, he thought—just had to try it and was instantly shot down in a hail of gunfire. Mary Caffiter screamed. The man backed into the saloon once more, slamming the door shut and hitting the floor as bullets from the street crashed through the windows, hurling shards of glass everywhere.

"Ruff!" Taylor Cribbs called out.

"Stay down. Stay here and stay down."

He tossed her Green's captured Remington revolver and kicked open the barred back door. He was met by sniper fire. Justice pulled his head back quickly as bullets punched through the doorframe and ricocheted around the storage room.

Ruff waited until the sniper fired again, and then he squeezed off from the floor. The big .56 rattled through the night, its bullet tracking toward the muzzle flash in the trees beyond. A man screamed, and Justice fired again.

The sniper quit screaming.

Behind Justice someone approached on the run. Justice got to his feet, turning quickly.

"Get him?" McCulloch asked.

"One of them."

"Head for the trees," the mayor of Deadwater said. "I'll cover you."

Justice looked at the big man and nodded. Taking a deep breath, he sprinted toward the oak trees across the alley, drawing a single, wild shot.

McCulloch made his try then. He ran like a bull—heavily, clumsily. Max Cord slammed the door shut behind him and locked it again.

Ruff Justice only saw a portion of what happened next. A Dan Court raider loomed up in front of the stumbling, newly elected mayor, and McCulloch was slow getting his gun up.

From beside a mammoth oak, a scattergun cut loose, spewing flame and death, and the raider was blown into bloody fragments.

Reloading hastily, Felipe Ortega stepped out to meet McCulloch.

"Thanks, marshal," McCulloch said with a crooked grin, and Ortega just stared at him.

"What are they doing, Felipe?" Justice asked.

"I don't know. I saw them taking up positions—there's at least two men in the hotel. I saw them open up at the meeting. What they have in mind, I don't know."

"I sure as hell do," McCulloch shouted. "Look!"

The town was on fire. It had started near the blacksmith's barn and had now spread to the empty saloon next door.

"If that keeps spreading, there won't be any town left," McCulloch said. "Christ. Shortest tenure as mayor in history. Justice—let's get the bastards."

It was a hell of an idea; *how* was a different matter. Working their way back toward the street, the three men stumbled onto a piece of luck.

Three raiders were riding fast down the main street, like cowboys hurrahing a hick town, firing into buildings at random.

That didn't last long. Justice shouldered the thunder gun, and his .56 blew one of the raiders from his saddle. His shot was echoed by Ortega's shotgun and McCulloch's pistol.

A horse reared up, and a bloody-faced man, illuminated by firelight, hit the ground to be dragged the length of the street as his boot caught in the stirrup. The third man made his escape, despite a second and third round fired through the barrel of the Spencer repeater.

And then the street was silent. Amazingly silent.

There was only the ominous crackling of flames as the fire spread up Main Street. A fire they had no chance of fighting.

When the flames began to lick at the walls of the coveted general store, the saloon door burst open, and Harry Green burst from the Red Dog in a manic fury.

"Bastards, bastards!" he shouted. He took a shot at what?—the flames, the night—and was answered by gunfire from the upper hotel windows.

Green went down, to lie writhing on the dirt of Main Street.

Justice and Ortega answered the gunfire with their own barrage of lead. McCulloch's gun was strangely silent. When Justice finally glanced at the mayor of Deadwater, he was slumped in the alley, half sitting against the wall of a nearby building beside them.

"I . . . same arm . . ." McCulloch said, and then he

passed out, the blood flowing freely from his injured shoulder.

Justice crouched down, whipped off his scarf, and tied off the artery. McCulloch groaned something and lay still.

"Dead?" Felipe asked.

"No. Let's try getting him back in the saloon. Back door."

Before they could manage to hoist McCulloch, they witnessed an amazing event. Green still lay in the middle of the street, badly injured. Now the door to the Red Dog burst open, and a figure emerged.

"His son," Ortega said, but it wasn't Green's son. It was Max Cord who worked his way across the street in a crouch, firing with his handgun into the windows of the hotel opposite. Still firing, he bent and grabbed his rival by the collar and started dragging him back toward the safety of the saloon.

Ruff and Ortega opened up, showering the hotel with buckshot and death-dealing .56 slugs. Three windows were blown out of the upstairs rooms, and the snipers yanked their heads back, diving for cover.

"He's going to make it," Ortega shouted, and then Max Cord was hit on his upper thigh. He was spun around, his leg taken from under him. The storekeeper got on hands and knees, however, and dragging Green behind him, somehow managed to make it into the Red Dog.

"Son of a bitch," Ortega said respectfully. "What in hell made him do that?"

"It's their town," Ruff Justice answered.

Ortega just shook his head. "Let's get McCulloch inside."

The front door was out of the question; the guns had opened up again. They dragged McCulloch through the alley and up to the back door, carrying him in as Gadsen watched, his eyes wide and fearful.

The women had placed Green on the bar and were trying to convince an angry Max Cord to follow suit. "I'm damned if I'll check out of this. Give me my gun, I'll show 'em," Cord argued.

"Another one?" Susan Donner asked as McCulloch was carried in. "Justice, have they got us beaten?"

"Not yet."

"Damn right, not yet!" Max Cord shouted. "They can't come in here shooting up our people . . ." And then Cord passed out, too. His pant leg was sodden with blood.

Susan looked at Ruff with beseeching eyes. Her town, her dream, was going up before her eyes, and there seemed to be nothing anyone could do to stop it.

Justice turned and started out again.

"Ruff!"

Ortega was at his side. Neither man looked back. "What do you want to do?" Felipe asked.

"I'm going to get them out of that hotel," Ruff Justice answered. "They've got us pinned down."

"Just how," Felipe asked with the slightest of smiles, "do you propose to do that?"

"Take it to them," Justice said. He had considered letting the fire spread to the hotel, encouraging it, but that would mean destroying even more of Deadwater—a town that was apparently in its death throes already. Rejecting that means of driving the raiders out left only one other—head-on.

"I'm going on in."

"You are mad, Justice!"

"Maybe. I'll take any better suggestions."

But Felipe had none. He shrugged. "What do you want me to do?"

Justice gave him the Spencer. "Keep their heads down. Give them something to think about. I'll try the back."

"They'll be watching for it."

"Then we won't disappoint them."

Felipe shrugged. "How much time do you want?"

"Give me five minutes before you start shooting. Then give me all the cover you can."

"All right. Justice—I won't be able to tell you from anyone else. Stay away from the front windows, eh?" Felipe smiled and levered a round into the breech of the thunder gun.

Justice slapped his shoulder and started circling back, moving away from the saloon through the night-shadowed oaks.

He moved warily through the trees, knowing that Court might have left some men out there—knowing that the Apache was somewhere nearby as well.

Distant shots rang out—not from the .56, not yet—and flames arced against the sky. Now the fire appeared to be more smoke than heat; the soft red glow above the town was cooling. Maybe Deadwater would be lucky yet. Or maybe Deadwater was a doomed town, a ghost town that should have been left to die.

Justice circled behind the stable and came face-to-face with a Court raider. The man had been looking up the street and not behind him. Now he heard a leaf crushed underfoot and turned, bringing his rifle around. But he was too slow, as the catlike figure of Ruff Justice struck.

The silver blade of Justice's bowie slashed out and found throat muscle, arteries, and trachea. The raider went down with a small, frightened whimper and lay dead against the dark, fire-shadowed earth.

Ruff worked his way toward the alley behind the hotel. There was a man at the back door. Now and then Ruff could see the shadowy figure moving behind the inches-wide gap where the door stood open. Ruff didn't plan to try the door. He had something else in mind.

Easing down the alley, staying close to the hotel wall, he looked up at the open window of the room he had slept in. The stacked barrels were still in place, and Justice clambered up and reached the ledge, throwing a leg up and over.

Then, moving cautiously, he slipped inside the empty room.

He paused, Colt in hand, listening.

He could hear voices, distant and muffled, and then the clacking of bootheels along the hallway.

Then the thunder gun opened up, Ortega peppering the windows of the hotel with .56 caliber bullets. Glass broke, and someone let out a startled curse. There seemed to be a lot of confusion—men dashing for cover, others shouting for them to get back to the windows.

Justice opened the door an inch or two and peered out. A bullet came through a front window to slam into the wall beside Ruff's head, tearing plaster loose and shaking the wall. That would be a bloody irony, to be tagged by his own rifle.

Justice stepped out into the hall, and with his Colt beside his leg, started walking toward one of the opposite rooms.

A raider rushed up the stairwell, and in the darkness he was uncertain—no one else but one of Court's men *could* be in the hotel, but he didn't recognize this tall man.

"Bob . . . ?" he said cautiously, his gun coming up simultaneously.

Ruff Justice fired from the waist, and his Colt sent a bullet smashing through the raider's face. The man toppled back to slide down the stairs, his strangled cry lost in the roar of the pistol shot.

A cloud of gunpowder smoke, acrid and dark, drifted down the hallway as Justice kicked open a door and stepped in to find two men at the window. One rose, half turning, as the other fired from his kneeling position. Justice fired into the kneeling man's chest, and the man was nailed to the wall by the spinning .44 slug. The raider's own shot was wide, whistling past Ruff's ear to ricochet off the doorframe.

The second man had taken too much time deciding what to do. He had risen and turned, and Justice put two rounds into the raider's body without hesitation. The man twitched crazily and went up on his toes. Then, as a third bullet took him high on the shoulder, he toppled over through the shattered window behind him to fall to the street below, where he lay twisted and still.

The night was suddenly quiet. Ruff could hear no movement in the hotel. The thunder gun had fallen silent. There was only the crackling of the flames and the heavy breathing of the tall man in buckskins.

Justice wiped back his long dark hair, thumbed fresh shells into the gate of the Colt, and started on, moving from room to room with utmost caution, toeing open doors, waiting, listening.

It took fifteen minutes before Justice had determined that there were no more Court men in the hotel. The others had either been outside or had hotfooted it when the battle began upstairs. Someone had left a cup of coffee and whisky on the kitchen counter.

Justice crossed the darkened hotel to the front door. The flames were painting the street orange and deep crimson. He opened the door very slowly, standing to one side.

"I'm coming out!" he shouted.

"Justice?" It was O'Hara from the saloon.

"That's right. Hold your fire."

"What's happening?" O'Hara called back, but Justice didn't answer him.

"Ortega!"

"Yes, Justice."

"Tuck that Spencer away."

Then he stepped out. The wind was blowing, the fire burning. He crossed the street, passing a dead raider, and entered the saloon. Ortega met him with a grin, handing back the big .56 repeater.

"Any luck?" the Mexican asked.

"We did all right. There's more of them out there— five of them by my calculations."

"Dan Court?" Ortega asked.

"Didn't see him. He's gotten away for now."

"We beat 'em, by God!" O'Hara shouted. Most of the others just looked stunned and worried, still frightened.

Taylor Cribbs walked the length of the room and wrapped her arms around Justice's waist, resting her cheek against his chest.

"How's McCulloch and Green?" Ruff asked her.

"They'll make it, I hope. Tinker's dead. Ruff . . . is this over yet?"

Justice looked into her eyes and shook his head. "Afraid not. Not until we kill Dan Court. He'll want his revenge now."

Looking across Taylor's shoulder, Ruff saw **Susan** Donner, her face pale and pained.

Their eyes locked for a moment, and then **Justice** turned away.

"Let's get that damned fire put out!" he said. **"You** people want this town to burn to the ground?"

16

The night was long, fire-swept and, exhausting. Men with rifles stood guard on the rooftops while a bucket brigade tried to douse the flames which threatened to devour Deadwater.

It wasn't over until nearly sunrise. Then Justice leaned back against a wall, his smoke-darkened face drawn and haggard, his arms weary, his lungs still filled with smoke and soot.

The town's third saloon was nothing but a collection of charred timbers, creaking and swaying in the wind—a structure of burned matchsticks ready to collapse. In the morning they would knock it down.

The blacksmith's barn was gone. The forge and anvil stood there untouched, but that was all that remained. The eastern wall of the hotel was badly charred, but the fire hadn't damaged the framing— the hotel could be repainted, scraped, and cleaned up.

"We saved more than we lost," Susan Donner said. She was beat, her hair knotted back carelessly, her dress smudged and singed.

"We were lucky."

"They were all working together, Justice—don't

you see? There's hope yet. When Court came into town, they pulled together. When the fire needed to be put out, they came together. Max Cord and Harry Green have agreed to try working out a partnership at the general store—Green couldn't believe it when they told him who had saved his life."

"Tinker's dead."

"Yes, yes he is, but Gadsen and O'Hara have decided that perhaps there is room for two men in the hotel business. Maybe seeing the town nearly destroyed has made them realize what they almost lost."

"Maybe. Hope so," Justice said. He was beyond gaining a fresh confidence in mankind just because of a single good act, or two. Anytime you started to feel hope for man, he came up with some new savagery— some new dark and evil scheme.

"You're tired," Susan said, touching his arm briefly. "Everyone's tired."

"I'm tired. There's another chore still to be done, though. We'll have to bury the dead."

"It'll be dawn soon," Susan replied, looking east.

"It'll be dawn—that's the time for burying."

"What will he do next, Justice? What will Dan Court try?"

"I don't know, but he'll be back. I'm afraid there's only one way to stop him, and that's kill him."

"Why doesn't he just give up?" she said in exasperation. "Why doesn't he just give up and move on before someone else gets killed!"

"He's not built that way. He likes to hurt people. He needs to get even."

"I'll let you get to work. God help this town— baptized in blood and fire!" She shook her head. "Do what you have to do, Justice, and then get some sleep.

Do me a favor though, come by the ranch tomorrow. . . . Bring your woman friend, if you want. Come by and get some decent food in you. I'll show you around the place."

She was going to say something else, but her mouth tightened and she turned away, mumbling something under her breath as she stalked toward the saloon and her waiting horse.

"What now?"

Felipe Ortega, looking fresh except for his smoke-stained clothing and smudged face, appeared beside Justice, watching Susan swing aboard her blue roan and ride out of town. She suddenly stung the roan with her quirt, and it leapt into a startled run.

"I think maybe she has feelings for you, Ruff Justice," Ortega said.

"Maybe." Maybe she still did after all. He turned to Ortega. "Let's get some shovels from McCulloch's stock and do the dirty work."

Ortega nodded silently. McCulloch, in high spirits despite his badly wounded arm, found two round pointed shovels and handed them over.

"I'd help if I could," the mayor of Deadwater said. "Since I can't—I'm going to sleep. Wish Mrs. Schoendienst had had time to get the restaurant opened up."

"Is that what she's going to do?"

"Oh, yeah. We kicked things around a little more last night. She's going to open it up as soon as she can get supplies. Couple of the other ladies are going to work with her . . . that Taylor Cribbs woman, I hear," McCulloch added.

He waited for a response from Justice but got none. Ruff ripped the paper off the head of the shovel and inclined his head. Ortega and Ruff walked slowly off toward their unhappy chore as the red sun broke free of the horizon and dully illuminated the smoke-shrouded town.

It was a wearying job, getting those men planted beneath the oaks. Justice stripped off his buckskin shirt as the sun rose higher. The two men worked in silence for the most part; it's hard to say much in the presence of the dead.

The last spadeful of earth covered the grave of Tinker, and Felipe straightened up, holding his back. He ran his wrist across his perspiring forehead, looked at it, and spoke.

"What now, Justice? What do we do next?"

"I'm going hunting," Ruff answered.

"Dan Court?"

"That's right," the scout replied. "Why wait for the man to make his plans, pick his time, maybe gather more people?"

"And so you are going to look for him, to strike first?"

"That's about it."

"*Bueno.* I will go with you."

"No you won't, Felipe."

"But yes, I will, Ruff Justice."

"It's not up to you to do this."

"No?" Felipe smiled. "I am the marshal of Dead-water, Justice, not you. I think it is my job if it is any-one's. Now, if you want to come with me . . ." He shrugged.

Justice was silent for a minute. Then he smiled, too. "All right. I'll go with *you.* Let's get this cleaned up, Felipe. I've a long way to go home, and I'm getting the feeling it's time for me to go."

"The ladies . . ."

"The ladies will do fine."

"Strange man, Justice," Ortega said. "With two such as those, I would do anything to linger here."

"Maybe," Justice said cryptically, "that's why I'm leaving as soon as possible."

"After we take Dan Court."

"After that," Justice said.

"Justice . . . did you see him?" Ortega asked. He was leaning against his shovel handle, his eyes on the distances.

"Court? Who do you mean, Felipe?"

"Not Court. I mean the one who was watching us as we worked."

"Who?"

"I don't know. An Indian, it seemed. An Apache—where I lived there are many Apaches. I thought an Apache. I saw him from the corner of my eye, but when I looked again, he was gone. Like a puff of smoke."

"An Apache." Justice looked into the forest, seeing nothing, hearing nothing—*knowing* still that Felipe Ortega was right. The Apache had been there.

"What does he want, Justice?" the Mexican asked.

"Death. My death, Felipe. Come on, let's put these shovels up and get us some tools that'll be of more use against Dan Court."

"We would be better off to sleep for just a little while, Justice."

"Let Court sleep. I want him now. I want this done with, Ortega."

"Yes," Felipe replied gravely, "I too want this done with. I want to rid the town of Court, to begin the rest of my life."

The town was still. One man—O'Hara—stood silent watch atop the hotel. Most of the others—wearied, bruised, and wounded, had fallen onto their beds and into a deep sleep. Justice hoped Court had done the same, that he planned no immediate attack.

Ruff Justice also wanted to get on with the rest of his life, and that meant that Court had to be hunted down and eliminated. He washed his face at the pump outside the Red Dog, rinsing the soot and dirt from his flesh, rinsing his red, weary eyes, combing back his long, dark hair with damp fingers.

Ortega had brought their horses from the stable, and Justice swung aboard the spotted pony, taking his Spencer rifle from Felipe.

The town slept. It smelled of ashes and of life. Deadwater was teetering on the brink of survival or destruction.

Felipe Ortega led the way up the sleeping street, as empty and still as the main street of a ghost town.

Or so it seemed. Justice saw one person up and awake aside from O'Hara. The tall redheaded woman stood in the window of the hotel, watching as Ruff Justice rode out of Deadwater and into the pine-crowded hills beyond.

They moved slowly through the morning, walking their horses amongst the pines and cedars, pausing frequently to listen, to watch. Court was out here—somewhere, but where? In the trees, Justice guessed, where there was good cover. But not too far south where he would be in sight of the cowboys working Susan Donner's ranch. Not too far east where he would be close to the Swamp Cheyenne reservation. But not too far from the town so he would be near enough to strike swiftly when he was ready.

Ortega found the hoofprints.

"Dan Court," Felipe said. He crouched against the earth and looked farther west to where the tangled hills broke away into a chaos of badlands.

159

Ruff swung down. The tracks showed four horses, moving single file toward the badlands, all of them shod, all moving with some degree of weariness. Justice agreed.

"Has to be."

"That is bad country they're riding into, Justice."

"I've been in there before; it's murder. Broken hills and tangled canyons. Not much water."

"Is he running now? He's riding farther than I thought he would."

"Maybe," Justice said, rising to dust off his hands and stare toward the distant, haze-shadowed badlands. "Maybe he's decided to run, but it's not going to do him any good. I'm still going after him."

"The two of us."

"That's a long way from Deadwater, marshal," Justice pointed out.

"Not so far that he can't ride back in one day and finish what he started." Ortega's face was solemn. "I want him as much as you do, Ruff Justice. The people back there—they asked me to do a job for them. I mean to do it."

They spoke no more of it. They both had a job to do. They owed it to the territory to finish off the Court gang—like a roving band of hostile Indians, Court's men had become nothing but killers, arsonists, and murderers.

They walked their horses toward the badlands which lay before them, red and eroded, cut bizarrely by wind and water. The pines fell away, and stunted pinyon and wind-twisted cedars replaced them. Aside from these occasional stunted trees and the gray willows in the washes, there was little vegetation.

The day dragged on; dust and heat plagued them.

The horses were weary, the men red-eyed with lack of sleep. At sunset they were rewarded.

At sunset they found Dan Court's camp. And more sign. Indian sign.

Felipe hadn't spotted it at first, but Justice, always wary in wild country, had. They reined up on the bluff overlooking an eroded, layered canyon which wound away to the south, toward the Flame. "Felipe," he said very quietly, "better keep your rifle ready."

"Court's camp . . ." Felipe gestured toward the west where both men had seen smoke rising before the dully glowing, descending sun.

"Cheyenne. Stone Eyes's people," Justice replied.

They had left their tracks against the bare red earth. Ten ponies in all, the remnant of the band which had attacked the wagon train.

"*Madre de Dios,*" Felipe whispered.

"What do you think? Want to turn back?"

Justice was looking out across the badlands into the reddish sun, his face lean and shadowed. Felipe looked at Ruff and started his horse forward into the red canyon. Justice slipped the beaded sheath from the Spencer and tucked it away. He found his buckskin sack filled with fresh .56 caliber cartridges and hooked it by its thong over the pommel of his saddle.

Then he started down the winding canyon after Felipe, riding toward the sun-stained badlands beyond.

They rode toward the smoke, which now rose against a purple sky as the shadows crept out from the base of the lone peak ahead and pooled darkly in the cuts.

They had lost the Cheyenne tracks, but Ruff couldn't worry about that just then. He could only hope the Indians had continued to drift.

But he knew they hadn't. The tracks were fresh, and the Cheyenne would be making night camp soon. There would be no huge, smoky fire as Court's men had constructed. Their camp would be well hidden, but they were around.

Justice had counted on making a war against five or six men—bad odds. Now he had not only Court's people to worry about but ten Cheyenne raiders. It didn't exactly flood a man with confidence.

They scrambled up out of the canyon, their horses kicking up dust and showering the bottom with rocks. Felipe looked back, both anguish and amusement visible on his dark face.

They were far from being a silent force.

The hills bunched together now, forming labyrinths and obstacles. They were time-eroded as well— bleakly shaped, grassless, and dark against the fading sunset.

Beyond the hills they found the camp.

No one seemed to be moving there, but four or five dark figures were huddled around what was now a dying campfire. A horse whinnied and Justice tensed, but Court's people paid no attention. The animal smelled some of its own kind on the hill above the camp, and a Cheyenne would have taken this warning to heart. Dan Court's people were too tired or too inexperienced or too confident to heed this warning.

Justice looked at Felipe, and the Mexican nodded. They slid from their horses' backs and ground hitched them, starting ahead on foot down the purple velvet of the wash toward Dan Court's camp.

17

They had no plan to kill all of those below. Justice and Felipe had talked that over. What they wanted was to take Court and the raiders if possible, return them to Deadwater, and let Deadwater have its first trial by jury.

That was the idea. But it was doubtful that Court would cooperate. Given the choice of being hung and being shot quickly, desperate men generally chose the bullets.

Justice didn't care which course Court chose. What did concern him was the knowledge that the shots would probably make the Cheyenne come looking.

Then what would they do with five prisoners and two guns against a band of hostiles? You couldn't run, so likely you stood your ground and fought. And died. There wouldn't be any help coming from anywhere. Fort Lincoln was impossibly distant, and there was no one else close by to count on.

Justice eased forward on his belly through the thin screening of greasewood and sage. He was within fifty feet of the outlaw camp when he stopped and sighted experimentally on one of the outlaws. Then he settled in to wait as Felipe, circling, took up his own position.

An owl cut a low swooping silhouette against the night sky, screeching as it dove. The first bright star appeared in the pale western sky. Justice watched the camp, feeling the night breeze against his cheek, which trickled perspiration.

He could smell fire—but it wasn't Court's fire—and meat cooking. The Cheyenne were that close. The first shot was sure to bring them on the run. . . .

And then the first shot rang out. Felipe had somehow given himself away or run into a sentry. The first shot flashed against the dark background of the hills, a red dragon's tongue flicking out at the night. That shot was immediately answered by a second lance of flame, and then the men in the camp below scrambled for cover.

Justice fired once and took a man down before he had fully risen. The guns turned on him—which was what he had wanted.

Ruff didn't know if Felipe was wounded, exposed, or down. He knew he himself was fairly well concealed, lying flat against the ground; let them train their fire on him.

And they did, half a dozen Winchesters and handguns throwing lead out into the night. They were firing wildly, desperate shots which sang off the rocks and flew into the air.

And some which came too damned close.

Dan Court. Justice saw the big man, identified him at last. He tracked onto him with the bead sight of the big .56 and squeezed off.

It was a miss. Court had either stumbled or hurled himself instinctively to the ground. Justice's shot clipped brush above the outlaw.

The shots Ruff was drawing were too close and too many for comfort. He began to move. Rolling toward a shallow that was on his left, he began working his way down toward the camp.

He didn't get far. An outlaw came panting up the slope, rifle in hand. He looked back fearfully and then rushed directly on toward Ruff.

Justice turned his rifle, crouched, and waited.

When the Court raider had nearly passed him, Justice rose, swung his Spencer by the barrel, and clubbed the outlaw to the ground, smashing his nose.

The man lay motionless on the ground. Ruff Justice bound him with his own belt and scarf and started on ahead. The gunfire had nearly stopped. *Where was Felipe?*

In answer to that a rifle from the hill opposite fired once, picking out a target in the dark brush below. A man yelled in agony and then lay still. Maybe Felipe was injured, but he could still shoot.

Two raiders down, possibly three. How many to go? Justice thought three, but there was always a chance he had miscounted, and he didn't want to run into an extra man he hadn't expected. Three or four then, including Court.

The gunfire laced the night with red and then just as abruptly fell silent. Was Felipe moving to a new position? Maybe. Justice hadn't seen him, but someone below had seen something.

Meanwhile the Cheyenne would soon be on their feet, looking toward the outlaw camp, moving toward their ponies. Justice didn't like the idea of having an army at his back, but that was the situation.

Dan Court leaped from the bluff above Justice and drove him to the ground with his body. Ruff's rifle was slammed from his hand, ringing off the stone in the wash.

Court's face was a lunatic's in the starlight. A big

man, his rage had given him incredible strength. He slammed a fist into Ruff's face and pinwheeling lights went on in the back of Ruff's skull.

Justice managed to roll his head to evade a second overhand right as he drove his knee up savagely at Court's groin. It struck the base of his spine painfully, and Court, like some savage creature, roared in pain and fury.

Justice had Court's head now as the big man tried to shake him off. Justice dug his thumbs into the hollows beneath his ears, and Court rolled aside, unable to withstand the pain.

Court kicked out with his boot as Justice tried to get to his feet; the heel glanced off Justice's forehead. Ruff staggered back, and the big man came in, knife in hand.

Justice tried to kick out at Court's kneecaps, to cripple him, but Court was no easy target in the darkness. Justice's bowie came up in his right hand, and Court just grinned. Blood was leaking from his lips, and his hair was a tangled mat. His shoulders were wide and hunched as he stepped in and drove the blade of his knife toward Justice's gut.

Justice slapped the arm away and brought his own bowie up savagely. He caught only shirt and hide as Court turned half away, trying to smash his forearm into Ruff's face while spitting out a stream of wild curses.

Court was insane, Justice realized now. The man was mad, frothing mad, and he wanted only to kill. The man he wanted to kill most in the world was now before him, crouched and ready as Court swarmed in again, one arm ready to block Justice's bowie, the other drawn back, his knife curled in his hand, gleaming softly.

Ruff feinted, stepped right, and saw Court's blade flash by within inches of his face. Both men were panting now, circling on the uneven ground. Behind them an occasional shot rang out.

Ruff's foot came down on a rounded rock and he stumbled, falling backward. Court came in immediately, savage glee on his face, but Justice caught his sleeve and yanked hard. Court toppled forward, right onto the point of Justice's upward-slashing bowie knife.

The point of the blade ripped open abdominal muscle and tagged heart and lung. Ruff clutched Court to him, not wanting the dying man to have the freedom to swing his own knife again.

He clung to Court, pinning his arm to his side, feeling the man's twitching and trembling, the slow leak of hot blood which smeared them both. And then Court was motionless atop Justice. Motionless and dead.

Ruff lay there, breathing raggedly, watching the bright heedless stars against the dark sky. Then he grunted, rolled Dan Court's heavy body aside, and started down the gully.

Felipe was still having his own private war.

The gunfire had slowed as panic gave way to deliberation. Each side was waiting for a clear shot, both were dug in. Then Felipe did something to draw the enemy's fire, perhaps shaking a bush or tossing a stone down the bluff. Ruff never saw what drew the fire, but he saw the reaction.

Two rifles in the willow brush below opened up. Felipe fired back at the muzzle flashes but seemed to hit nothing.

Ruff moved in then, circling slowly, the Spencer

cool in his grip. Two men left. Not counting the one he'd left bound and gagged on the ridge.

Two men, and Justice knew where they were.

He slipped through the willow brush. The starlight threw long, interwoven shadows across the path he followed. He held the rifle down and leveled, and when he came up silently behind the Court raiders, he gave them their choice.

"Drop the guns or die," Ruff said mildly.

Both men froze. They glanced at each other, a message passing between their eyes.

"You've got a chance if you put them down," Justice told them.

"We've got a chance this way. . . ." The first man was spinning, throwing himself onto his back, firing up at the tall buckskinned figure behind him as his partner scrambled for deeper brush.

The raider had gone the wrong way at the wrong time, in front of the wrong man. He rolled onto his back and tried to fire from the ground at Ruff Justice, but Ruff had the Spencer shouldered and sighted, and his buffalo gun spoke with deadly authority.

The second man, panicked, began crashing through the brush as he fled. Justice started after him. Felipe would have heard the shots and known that it was Justice down there—the .56 sounded nothing like the outlaws' Winchesters, which had a report like a flat crack. When the .56 spoke, it was unmistakable. Felipe would be holding his fire.

That left only the single fleeing raider to worry about, and Ruff broke into a jog, weaving through the starlit willows.

He could hear the frantic panting ahead, the snapping brush as the outlaw tried to fight his way to freedom. He didn't make it.

Justice caught up with him in a small sandy clearing. A screen of sage and willow brush rose all around them to head-height.

"You can still throw it down," Justice told the fleeing outlaw, who stopped, his body heaving with exertion.

The man spun, his rifle coming up. "You can go to hell!" he shouted. But it wasn't Ruff who would make that last terrifying trip into the darkness of the underworld—it was the raider.

Except Justice had never fired his weapon.

The outlaw glanced at Justice, nodded his head crazily, and tried to look behind him. The Cheyenne arrow was imbedded in his spine.

The warrior burst from the brush to Ruff's right, and another emerged from the willows to Justice's left. *This is it,* he thought. There wasn't time to get both of them. Ruff took the nearest man, the one on his right, firing into the Indian's body. He saw the Cheyenne tumble and sprawl, heard an echo of his own shot to the left and spun back.

The second Cheyenne lay dead on the ground.

"Thanks, Felipe," Justice said, but it wasn't Felipe Ortega who emerged from the brush.

"Ortega took some lead. He's still back on the ridge," Tom Beers said, walking forward, his repeater in his hands. He ejected the empty cartridge from his Winchester and grinned. Tucking his rifle under his arm, he began rolling a smoke.

"Where in hell did you come from?" Ruff asked, going down on one knee to rest.

"We heard the shooting. We've been chasing down these Cheyenne all day. Stole some beef, killed a hand. Me, Slick, Esteban, and Miguel Andojar trailed after them. We got six for sure; the rest are scattered and traveling fast."

"Any of you get hurt?" Ruff asked.

"Only Slick—got his ear shot off. He don't want to talk about it, says it spoils his good looks. I wouldn't mention it."

Ruff rose, smiling. He walked to the Indians, making sure they were dead. Stone Eyes would be short a few soldiers in his next holy war.

"I left one up on the ridge," Justice told Tom Beers.

"Let's round him up then. Maybe the folks in Deadwater would like to have him."

The prisoner was dirty, bloodied, and enraged. They walked him back to where Miguel and Esteban were hunched over Felipe Ortega. Slick emerged from the brush a second later, a rag wrapped around his head.

"Wanted to make sure who you were," he explained.

"How's Felipe?"

"All right, I expect, barring complications. One through the butt, one in the foot. He's luckier than some," Slick pointed out. At least, he was thinking, Felipe's looks weren't ruined.

"Can you make it, Felipe?" Ruff asked.

"Home?" he asked, and it was the first time Justice had ever heard someone call Deadwater home.

"Home."

"*Si*, help me up. I have seen enough of the badlands, enough of fighting, enough of war and blood. Take me home, Ruff Justice."

Beers and Esteban helped Justice get Felipe to his feet and onto the back of his recovered horse. Then, with the captured raider in tow, Ruff lifted his hand to Susan Donner's crew and started back toward the distant, dark town of Deadwater.

They rested frequently on the trail. The outlaw glowered at them, sullen and silent. Maybe he wished he'd been killed after all. He didn't have much to look forward to.

It was dawn when they reached Deadwater again, the late moon rising in the pink and orange sky.

"Listen," Ortega said. He was hunched forward, in pain, but he could still smile. Ruff listened and nodded. They heard hammers ringing, saws at work. Deadwater had become a town at last—a place where people built and raised families and made an honest living, sharing small pleasures and sorrows. Deadwater was coming to life; the new blood had taken awhile to work, but now it was working at last.

With first light men and women had risen, stretched, yawned, and suddenly realized that they had things to do that day—rebuild, transfer goods, clean up, open for business.

Ruff and Felipe rode down the main street with the prisoner behind them, and people called out or waved, walking toward them to ask with concern about Felipe's wounds. They were Ortega's friends, his neighbors. He had come home.

And Ruff Justice's job was finally over.

18

Sunrise was a wildly flourishing rose in the eastern skies. Ruff Justice yawned and stretched, glanced at the hotel room window, and was surprised to see that the sun hadn't fully risen yet.

"Nearly twenty-four hours," Taylor Cribbs said.

Ruff blinked, looked at the naked woman standing at the window, and asked her to repeat what she had just said.

"You've been asleep for nearly twenty-four hours. Except for the two hours when you stirred last night around midnight and woke *me* up. You probably don't even remember it. Probably thought it was a dream."

"It was much too vivid and memorable," Ruff Justice lied, "for me to ever make that mistake." Taylor smiled then, and it was all right. All right that he had absolutely no recollection of making love to this strapping, lovely woman.

She crossed the room and perched on the edge of the mattress, stroking Ruff's head, letting her fingers trail down across his hard-muscled chest.

"What now?" she asked after a long while.

"Now," he said, sitting up, swinging his bare feet to

the floor of the hotel room, "I'll be getting back to Bismarck."

"Bastard," Taylor half snarled. There were tears in her green eyes.

"What should I do, Taylor? Stay on as Ortega's deputy? Change the hotel linen? You've got a life here in Deadwater; I don't."

"You belong with the army."

"That's right." He was searching for his trousers among the sheets.

"Under the bed," Taylor said sharply. "I think you *were* asleep."

"Impossible." He recovered his buckskins from underneath the bed and started dressing.

"Back to the army—they need you so badly." When she got no response from Justice, Taylor went on. "Back where Indians and outlaws can shoot at you, where you can make sure that you die young and valiantly."

"Back there," was all Ruff Justice said. He walked to the mirror on the wall, poured water into the basin, and dug into his saddlebags for his ebony-handled straight razor. He began working his way carefully around his long drooping mustache with the honed blade of the razor. Taylor watched him in silence.

"What are you going to do?" Justice asked.

"Do you care?"

Ruff turned toward her. "Of course I do. You know I do, Taylor."

Her anger was subsiding. She shrugged and crossed the room, took her pale blue wrapper from the coatrack, and slipped it on.

"Fry eggs, I guess. Work for Mrs. Schoendienst. Serve drunks their coffee, take a few slaps on the fanny."

"Survive."

"Yeah," Taylor Cribbs answered with a crooked smile. "Just survive, Ruffin T. Justice."

"Which is all any of us do—if we're lucky," the man at the mirror said.

"Yeah." The woman was thoughtfully silent for a minute. Then she walked to Ruff and kissed him once deeply, holding his face in her hands. "Survive well, Ruff Justice."

There was nobody on the streets when Ruff rode out astride the spotted horse in the early morning light. It was just as well. They had begun a new life; he was no longer a part of it. There was no one he wanted to say good-bye to . . . except Susan Donner, and somehow he couldn't bring himself to ride down to the ranch. So he lifted the horse's head, pointed it toward the pines, and heeled it into a brief, exhilarating run.

The sun was golden flame behind the pines as Justice slowed his horse to a walk and watched as the squirrels and jays cavorted, bickering, pursuing one another through the trees.

He was still out there.

Justice knew it, felt it. The Apache was still there. Silent as the wind, a deadly, invisible hunter. He was still there, and he wanted to kill Ruff Justice. There wasn't much Justice could do at that point but wait for the Apache to make his move, knowing the Apache would very likely win this man-to-man battle. The Apache had the advantage of knowing where Justice was and knowing when he would strike.

Justice could do little but remain wary. He seemed to be nearly dozing in his saddle. His long body was relaxed, his hat tugged low, but he was alert to every subtle shadow, each sound. Leaves twisted by from a nearby oak, and Justice watched them sail earthward. His right hand was on his Spencer. He was as ready as he could make himself.

It didn't do him much good when the Apache hit him unexpectedly from directly overhead. The stalker leaped from the bough of a pine, and his body crashed into Ruff's, a knife flashing toward the scout's eyes.

It would have been over then, but the spotted horse panicked and reared up as the Apache landed on its back. Both men were spilled to the ground in a tangle of limbs.

Justice came up first, his bowie in his hand. The Apache's hands were empty. Ruff saw the knife lying on the ground ten feet away, too far to do the Apache any good.

"Might as well forget it," Ruff Justice said. "You've already gotten some money out of this—three hundred, isn't it? Why not take off and live to spend it."

The Apache didn't answer. He was half-crouched, his hands loose and flexing. Justice had never seen such a man; dark as any Indian, darker than some, he had expressionless blue eyes which never wavered.

His English was excellent. "I was paid to do this job. I'll do it. The others failed. I'm better than they were."

"Who paid you?" Ruff asked. "The lady in black?"

"I can't turn and walk away," the Apache said, ignoring Ruff's question.

"Sure you can, and you're a fool if you don't. Not many men get a chance to walk away from their own graves. I'm giving you that chance."

But there was no getting through to the Apache. He was a primitive thing—a warrior with a warrior's set of values. He had come to kill, and if he failed, it would be only because he had been killed himself.

Justice started forward, holding his bowie edge-up, blade ready for a slashing cut up through the bowels in case the Apache leapt at him.

But he wasn't going to do that. Some thought, some killing idea was still going through the Apache's mind, and what it was Justice didn't understand.

Until the Apache made his try.

His hands were incredibly fast. The right went behind his neck, and something clicked in Justice's mind. He had seen it once before, down on the Mississippi. He had seen a man who didn't know what was coming stand there and take it and die for it.

The Apache had a sheath behind his neck, suspended loosely enough for the maneuver of throwing a knife. Justice moved.

Ruff flung himself to the side as the Apache, fast as any gunhand, drew and threw the knife. It flashed through the air, missing Justice by inches, embedding itself in the pine behind him, and quivering there for a moment.

Justice kept rolling.

The Apache had dived for the thunder gun, the big .56 had hit the ground when they toppled from the horse. Now the gun, fired from one knee, bellowed out a savage warning. The bark of the tree behind Justice exploded in a shower of reddish fragments.

The Apache rose and fired again, but by then Justice had gotten behind the tree. The .56 caliber bullet tore a low hanging bough from the huge pine.

It was a bad shot, but the Apache wasn't used to the rifle; his weapon was a razor-edged throwing knife. Justice still had his Colt revolver. Now he poked his head out and drew a shot which again struck the tree, causing it to shudder, massive as it was.

Ruff's Colt spoke twice, and the Apache howled

with pain. He dropped the rifle and sprinted into the trees, holding his arm. Justice chased him with two more .44s but hit nothing.

The forest was silent then. The jays had quit their squawking, the squirrels their noisy chattering. The echoes of the gunshots drifted away, and there was nothing. Nothing but the two silent hunters, only one of whom would survive.

Justice began to walk quietly across the leaf-littered ground. His boots made only whispers of sound, his eyes searching right and left. The Colt's curved hammer rocked back as his finger poised on the cool blue steel trigger, ready to squeeze off a killing shot.

The Apache was gone again. The man was a ghost—a soundless, formless woods creature. A stalking cat.

But the cat was leaking blood, marking his trail through the pines. He could walk without making a sound over dead leaves, but he couldn't stop his blood from flowing.

Justice moved after him slowly. There was a crimson spot on a brown oak leaf, there another, and another. Ruff looked up toward the stack of lichen-covered boulders clustered on a low mound of earth beyond the line of trees.

But the Apache wasn't there. He had circled again, and he came from behind the twisted oak to Justice's left, a length of wood in his hand.

He lashed out, and as Justice turned, firing, the branch cracked against Ruff's wrist. The Colt discharged into the air and then fell spinning to the earth.

The Apache raised the club again, his face still expressionless, his eyes still empty. Ruff Justice's long leg came up, his boot smashing into the Apache's face before he could swing his crude weapon.

Justice saw the Apache stagger back and dove for his Colt. He recovered it and rolled to his feet—to find the Apache gone again, vanished on the wind.

Ruff took three deep breaths and started on slowly, inching through the woods. He realized now that he wouldn't have to track the man down. The Apache would return again and again, attacking, always attacking until one of them lay still beneath the pines.

Still the blood leaked onto the ground. More of it now. That .44 had ripped his arm up pretty good. Justice had a wounded cougar in front of him, somewhere.

The tracks led in a circle, and Justice understood suddenly that he had made an error. The Apache was moving back toward the horse, toward the thunder gun, toward his knives.

Justice's lip curled back. He was angry with himself; but then you expect a captured man to surrender, you expect a wounded man to make a run for it. You expect a beaten man to give it up.

The Apache was a different sort of man, and Justice wondered about his background. Where had he come from, who was he? Why the blue eyes? . . . He forced these thoughts from his mind and replaced them with thoughts of survival.

Justice turned and started at a jog trot toward the spotted horse.

The Apache beat him there.

Justice saw the man bent over the ground, saw his hand snatching up a knife. The rifle wasn't far away, but he wanted the knife. It was the Apache's tool of destruction, the one he preferred to do his murderous work with.

Justice slowed and walked into the clearing, his Colt close to his thigh in his dangling hand.

"That's no good now," Justice said quietly.

The Apache turned and straightened, the knife reversed for throwing in the palm of his hand. His blue eyes flashed.

"We are the same, you and me," the Apache said. "There's no difference between us, Ruff Justice."

"Not much."

"You are a warrior; you understand."

"I don't understand murder," Ruff answered.

"No!" Now there was emotion in the Apache's eyes. Anguish and a plea for understanding. "I am not talking about murder. I am talking about undertaking a job, agreeing to fight, finishing what I have started. I have watched you, Ruff Justice. You fight for wages too, but you do more than you must. You fight until the enemy is dead—or you are. You chased the outlaws into the badlands, knowing there were Cheyenne there. Nothing could stop you from doing your duty, a warrior's duty—we are the same."

"No, my friend. Nobody ever hired me to do murder. We're not the same at all."

"Look beneath the surface, look in your heart," the Apache replied. "It is there, this need to live violently. To die violently."

Then the Apache threw his knife, and it was a good throw. But Justice's Colt was quicker. Shifting to one side, he fired. The knife missed. Maybe it was luck, maybe the Apache's injuries had taken the edge off his marksmanship.

Maybe he had missed on purpose.

Ruff's .44 slug entered the Apache's shirt, making a small, round, smoldering hole in the white fabric. It ripped through his ribs, becoming a twisted, fragmented thing which ravaged heart and lungs and exited through the cavernous hole it tore through the Apache's back.

The man went down like a felled tree. He said nothing more, barely moved. One blue eye watched as Ruff Justice walked to him and stood over him with the smoking gun. There was an unrecognizable expression in that eye briefly, and then there was nothing—just a cold, blue, dead eye.

Justice stood there for a minute, hearing the jays begin their chattering, the squirrels darting across the leaf-littered forest floor. Then, shaking his head, he turned and went to where the spotted pony stood.

"Damn you!" the voice from the trees cried out. The voice was anguished, nearly hysterical. The lady in black emerged from the trees, wobbling on unsteady legs. Ruff glanced in that direction and then turned his attention to the spotted horse, soothing it.

"Damn you, Ruff Justice! Damn you to flaming eternal hell!"

Ruff turned slowly toward the lady in black.

"Aren't you getting a little tired of parading around in a lady's dress, Pete?"

Pete Conklin stopped and stood stock-still, staring through his dark veil at the tall scout in buckskins.

"You knew then."

"For some time," Justice answered.

"How?"

"Wiley Pabst told me, but I didn't put it together right away. I've never seen a little old lady scramble out of a hotel window and down an alley like you did back in Deadwater."

"I see."

"Why did you tag along anyway, Pete? Didn't you

trust these high-paid killers of yours to get the job done?"

"Should I have?" he asked bitterly.

"I don't know. Why do it at all? Why hire these men? Why not do it yourself, Pete?"

"With these?" Conklin ripped off his long black gloves and held up deformed, scarred, nearly flesh-less hands. They had been burned nearly to the bone. "Was I supposed to come up against you and try to outdraw you with *these*? I used to be good with a gun. I could have beat you. I could have beat Jud Hollister. It took me five minutes to set up the one shot I did take at you. I could hardly squeeze the trigger of that rifle."

"Tough."

"You don't understand at all, do you?"

"I understand you tried to kill me."

"My brothers and me. You burned that barn down around us. We didn't have a chance."

"As much chance as that Indian woman had, Pete."

"A squaw! What did you care about a squaw? Fire . . ." the man shuddered. "Do you know what it's like to be trapped in a fire, to hear your brothers scream-ing, to hear flesh crackling, to smell your own hide being seared? You did that to me. You!"

"No, Pete. You and your brothers did it when you took that Indian girl and killed her."

"Nobody else would've done what you did! Nobody else would roast people alive."

Justice was swinging aboard his horse. Conklin came a little closer. "What are you doing? You can't just ride off!"

"Sure I can. There's a couple of real ladies I want to see back in Bismarck."

"You don't even care! You don't care that my brothers are dead, that I'm crippled."

"Not much," Justice said after a moment's thought. "You want sympathy from me? Sympathy after you three raped and killed a young woman who was worth a hundred like you? Not likely. Tell me one thing though, Pete. Why the lady's getup?"

"Why! Why?" Conklin ripped the veiled hat from his head—from his yellowed, seared skull which had only a few tufts of white hair on it. His fire-gnawed face was the face of a gargoyle, of a monster. "Why do you think, Justice? Why do you think?"

Then Pete Conklin started to laugh. He laughed hoarsely through fire-scored lungs and throat, a wheezing, mad sound. "You can't ride away, you can't do this!" Conklin began to shout.

He looked around wildly until his dull eyes lighted on the knife still stuck in the big pine. He tore it from the tree with crippled hands and threw himself at Justice.

Ruff shot him.

The Colt slammed Pete Conklin back against the tree, and he sagged to the ground. Justice looked at the still-smoking Colt, wondering.

Wondering if he had done Pete Conklin one last, merciful favor.

He fished in his pockets and brought out the small pasteboard object. He flipped it away, and it sailed softly through the air to land on Conklin's dead, ravaged face. Jack of diamonds.

Ruff sat for a time looking past the treetops at the clear, blue sky. He shook his head once, then kneed the spotted pony forward. Toward Bismarck.

Toward Bismarck and the two lovely blond women there. He knew they could help cleanse his soul, wash a part of all this away. In a little while Justice was out of the trees. He couldn't see Deadwater or the dead men behind him, only the long empty plains ahead. It was plenty.

WESTWARD HO!

The following is the opening section from the
next novel in the gun-blazing, action-packed new
Ruff Justice series from Signet:

RUFF JUSTICE #26: TWISTED ARROW

The band struck up again, and the dancers moved out
onto the floor. The big man with the red beard was
pretty well drunk, and he glowered at them. The
band wasn't much, but it managed to fill Bismarck,
Dakota Territory's town hall, with plenty of noise.
Even if the tuba player did look like he was ready to
expire from the effort of forcing deep notes from his
huge, brassy instrument.

The celebration, if it could be called that, was for
the citizens of the town of Clear Creek—or rather the
survivors of Clear Creek. Stone Eyes, the Cheyenne
renegade, had burned the town to the ground, keeping most of its inhabitants in a state of siege for nearly
a week until the army had arrived, and killing or
wounding more than two dozen men and women.

Jake Troll was one of the survivors. He was big, red-
bearded and red-eyed, and he was staggering drunk.
He didn't like dances, he didn't like tuba music; he

especially didn't like the fancy dude who spun by with young Jenny Farnsworth in his arms.

Jenny was smiling brightly, her eyes alight with some emotion she had never displayed to Jake Troll, though Troll had been courting her for some time now.

"What the hell's that supposed to be?" Troll grumbled to his silent companion, a one-armed, rail-thin man called Skitch.

"What?" Skitch had his own drinking to do. His head came up slowly, and some sort of distant comprehension crept into his befuddled expression. "Him?" Skitch pointed to the tall man in the dark suit, string tie, ruffled shirt, and highly polished black boots. He wore his hair brushed down past his shoulders; his dark mustache drooped to his jawline. As the two men watched, he threw back his head and laughed heartily.

Jenny Farnsworth placed one gloved, demure hand over her lips in a vain effort to hold back her answering laugh.

"Him," Jake Troll nodded. "What in Christ's name is he supposed to be? Ruffles and lace, for Christ's sake. That supposed to be a man?"

Skitch took a thoughtful sip of his lemonade, which had a suspicious brown hue to it. He shook his head. "Don't you remember seeing him out there, at Clear Creek?"

"I had more important things to see at Clear Creek than some dude. I had Indians to look at."

Jake puffed up a little. He had killed his first man back there, an attacking Cheyenne warrior; you'd have thought he had made the plains safe forever.

"That's that army scout, Ruff Justice," Skitch reminded his bearded friend.

Jake Troll abandoned the pretense that he was sipping the Clear Creek Ladies Club's lemonade. He swigged his whisky from the bottle now, looking around belligerently to see if anyone had the nerve to say anything to him about it.

No one had any such intention. Jake Troll was a massive man, filled with a self-importance and meanness.

"That's my girl," he said in a deeply slurred voice. Skitch didn't even glance at him. "Jenny Farnsworth is my girl." Still Skitch didn't answer. It was best not to say anything at all to Troll when he got in these moods.

Skitch saw the tall man who was dancing with Jenny Farnsworth smile again. Then Ruff Justice bent his head a little and whispered something into her ear. She had a pretty, little, round pink ear, scrubbed and wholesome, and Skitch couldn't blame Justice for adding a little kiss to it as he drew away.

Jake Troll roared and slammed his bottle down on a nearby table, upsetting a flower arrangement the ladies had placed there. He stalked across the floor through the whirling dancers, his feet moving in time to the blasting of the tuba.

Skitch shook his head, sipped at his well-laced lemonade, and stood ready to watch the fun.

"You," Troll's voice boomed. "I want to talk to you."

Ruff Justice glanced at the big red-bearded man who stood hunched in the middle of the dance floor.

Then he led the light, pretty woman in his arms past the drunk in a graceful turning dance step.

Troll tried to put a hand on Justice's shoulder, but it wasn't that easy as the couple dipped and twirled away, still smiling and talking in low voices while the band worked valiantly on.

"Was he talking to me?" Ruff Justice asked.

"Who?" They were inside the town hall, but somehow there was starlight in Jenny Farnsworth's deep brown eyes. She held one of the tall army scout's hands in her own, while her other hand held his shoulder, lightly squeezing it from time to time.

They worked their way around the dance floor, leaving the red-bearded man to stand, bearlike, in the center of the room.

"Him," Ruff Justice said, inclining his head. "I thought he said something to me."

Jenny Farnsworth glanced that way, grimaced, and said, "Oh, that's just Jake Troll."

"Friend of yours?"

"He wants to marry me. He beats up any man who's nice to me." The girl shrugged.

"Fine," Justice said with a smile. "Jenny, you ought to tell me these things."

"It only happens when he's drunk. I didn't think he'd had time yet."

Ruff peered down into those brown eyes, wondering at her logic. But then it wasn't logic that attracted Ruff Justice to this one. The woman was young and compactly built, with an astonishing firmness of body. Jenny was full-breasted and eager to laugh, her mouth wide and sensual.

"You," a voice called from far away. This time

Justice ignored him. He didn't like drunks; he especially didn't like belligerent drunks. Most particularly he didn't like drunks who wanted to prove some point the day after Justice and the army had just completed a bloody, tedious, frustrating cat-and-mouse game with the elusive Stone Eyes. They'd had to drag the people of Clear Creek out of their razed town and rush them across the prairie to the safety of Bismarck.

But Jake Troll wouldn't let it go. The band staggered to a halt, and Troll's voice roared out in the sudden silence.

"I'm talking to you, tall man. Dude. I want to talk to you, boy. Outside."

"Oh," Jenny Farnsworth said in frustration, "I just didn't think he'd had time to get plastered!" Her tiny fists bunched, and she smiled ingenuously at Ruff, who turned, sized up his man, and answered.

"He's had time."

"Well then, you'll have to let him beat you up. Or," she added brightly, "you could shoot him."

"I could shoot him," Ruff repeated in wonder.

"I know you have a gun. It's in your holster. Right there." She tapped the holster and the little Colt New Line .41 which rode there. Ruff's town gun.

"You!" Troll bellowed. Heads turned, and people stood watching.

"Doesn't anyone ever grow up?" Justice muttered. "I'll be back," he told Jenny Farnsworth.

"Are you going to shoot him?" she asked a little too eagerly.

"Jenny, you're a darling, but I don't know about this side of you."

"In Clear Creek everyone always shot each other."

God, she was lovely. And she was very young.

"You!"

"I'll be back," Ruff said, patting her shoulder. "Save the next dance."

"Can't I watch?" Her eyes searched Ruff's, and he smiled a little uneasily.

"Not this time. I'll let you watch the next time I shoot somebody."

"Oh, thank you," she said, and Ruff began to wonder about the future of this relationship.

He turned away and walked toward the hulking, red-bearded figure who stood watching him, waiting. The band struck up again as Ruff Justice reached Troll.

"Outside," Troll said with malicious glee.

"I'll miss this dance."

"You'll miss more than that."

"Oh, Mr. Justice," a heavily powdered woman of fifty called, waving a handkerchief. "When are you going to sing for us?"

Troll's lips twisted contemptuously.

"Later, Mrs. Anderson," Ruff Justice called back.

"You sing for the ladies, do you?" Troll said. They were nearly at the door.

"Works wonders. But you wouldn't understand that, friend." Outside, the air was cool. Down the street Bismarck's saloons roared with activity. The stars were bright and close. "You know, Troll, this is a waste of energy and time. Why don't you wander off and find yourself something else to drink?"

"Why don't you go to hell! . . ." Troll threw a right-hand hook at Justice's head. It missed by a foot, Ruff had been anticipating the sucker punch. He pulled back his head, took Troll by his coatfront, and yanked him close, driving one knee up into the big man's groin.

Troll folded up with a sickening groan, and Ruff brought both interlocked hands up into the red-bearded man's face. Troll tottered backward, flipped over a hitching rail, and fell on the street to lie still and peaceful against the earth.

The scream from inside the dance hall brought Justice's head around sharply. He rushed inside as the band broke off in the middle of its number.

The crowd had gathered around something in the center of the dance floor; that something was a dead man. Ruff Justice pushed his way through.

He didn't know the man who was lying facedown on the floor, an arrow in his back. An arrow such as Justice had never seen.

It was fitted with crow feathers. Instead of being straight, the shaft was twisted, as if its maker had patiently taken growing arrowweed and tied it as it grew to form the odd shape. There was no paint on the arrow.

"Where in hell did that come from?" someone asked, but there was no answer. The recent Indian fears came back, and the survivors of Clear Creek glanced around nervously, some moving toward their weapons stored in the cloakroom.

"How could someone shoot Clive? God's sake, we'd have to have seen a man with a bow and arrow!"

But no one had, or no one remembered having seen anything. And at first no one noticed the dully shining, nearly round object lying near the dead man's hand.

It was left to Ruff Justice to crouch and pick it up. He turned it in the lantern light and let it gleam: it was Spanish, it was ancient.

It was gold.